FAR OUT
CLASSIC STORIES

STONE ARCH BOOKS
a capstone imprint

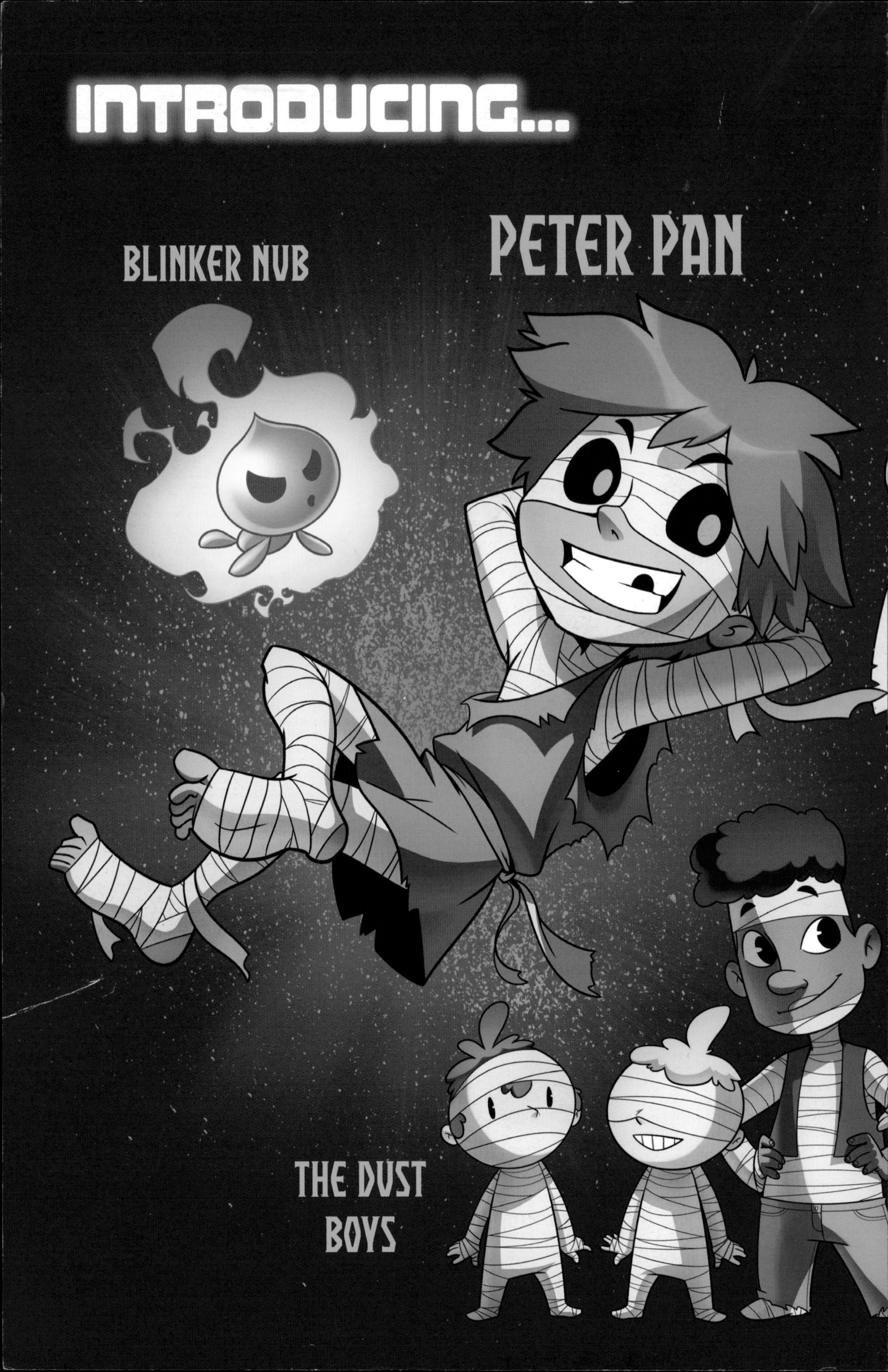
INTRODUCING...
BLINKER NUB
PETER PAN
THE DUST BOYS

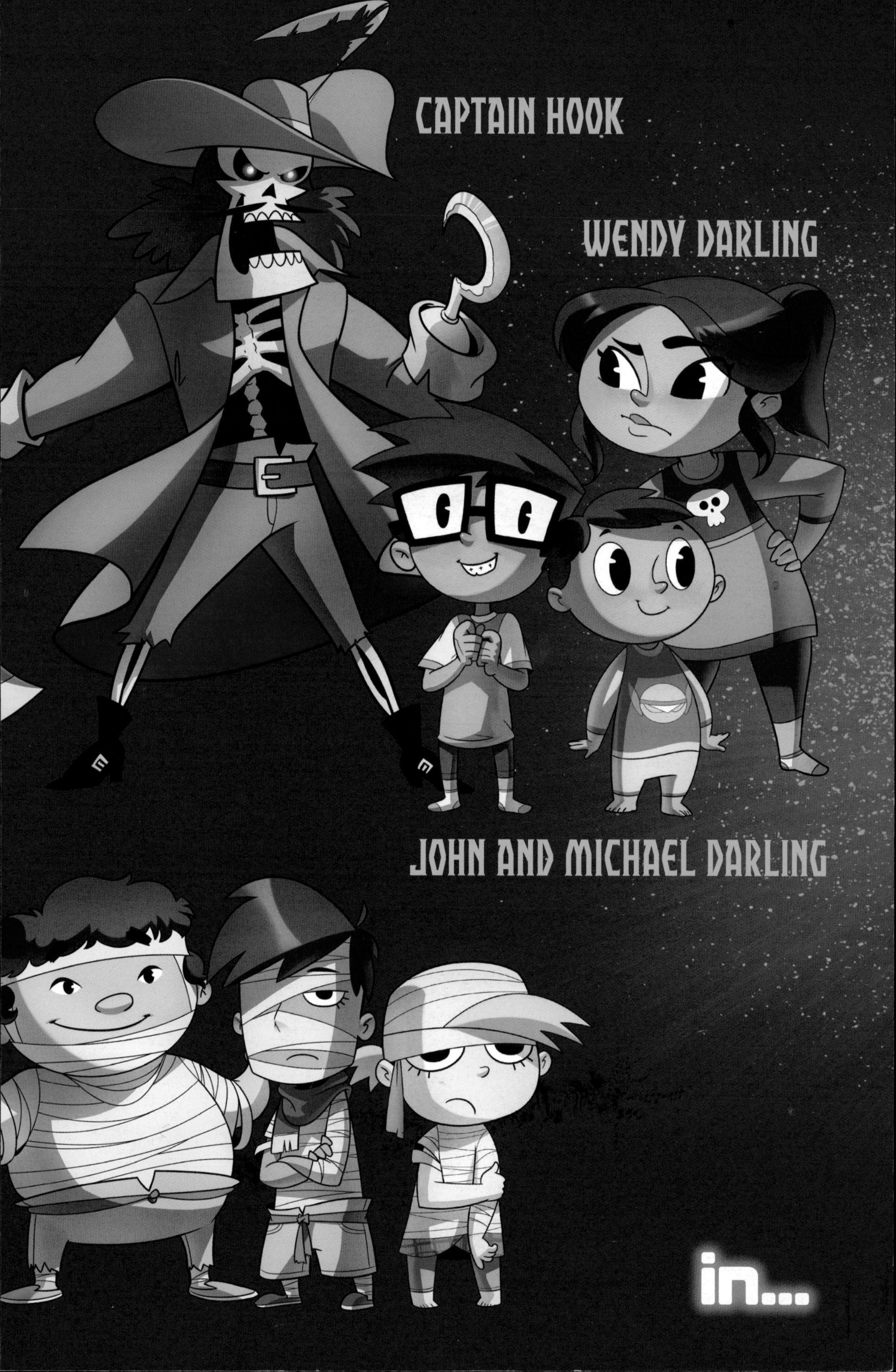
CAPTAIN HOOK
WENDY DARLING
JOHN AND MICHAEL DARLING
in...

Far Out Classic Stories is published by
Stone Arch Books,
an imprint of Capstone.
1710 Roe Crest Drive
North Mankato, Minnesota 56003
www.capstonepub.com

Library of Congress Cataloging-in-
Publication Data is available on the
Library of Congress website.
ISBN: 978-1-4965-8686-5 (hardcover)
ISBN: 978-1-4965-9193-7 (paperback)
ISBN: 978-1-4965-8687-2 (eBook PDF)

Summary: A boy named Peter Pan ran
off to a magically spooky place to
become . . . a mummy! After overhearing
Wendy Darling telling her brothers scary
stories, Peter brings them all to Mummy
Land too. But the island is filled with lots
of creepy creatures, including a skeleton
pirate who wants to put Peter in the
tomb once and for all!

Designed by Hilary Wacholz
Edited by Abby Huff
Lettered by Jaymes Reed

Printed and bound in the USA.
PA99

FAR OUT CLASSIC STORIES

PETER PAN IN MUMMY LAND

A GRAPHIC NOVEL

BY BENJAMIN HARPER

ILLUSTRATED BY FERN CANO

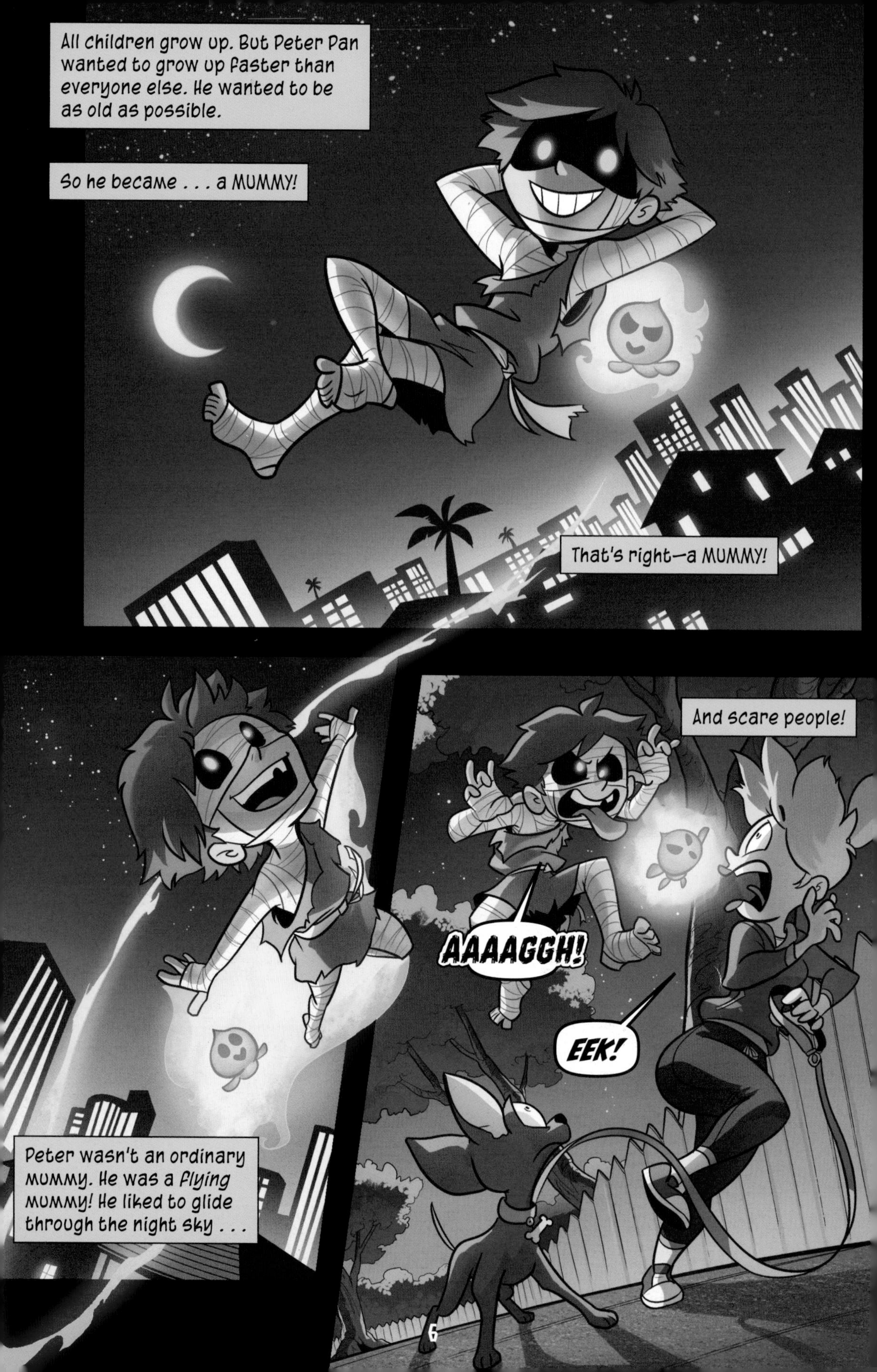
All children grow up. But Peter Pan wanted to grow up faster than everyone else. He wanted to be as old as possible.
So he became . . . a MUMMY!
That's right—a MUMMY!
Peter wasn't an ordinary mummy. He was a *flying* mummy! He liked to glide through the night sky . . .
And scare people!
AAAAGGH!
EEK!

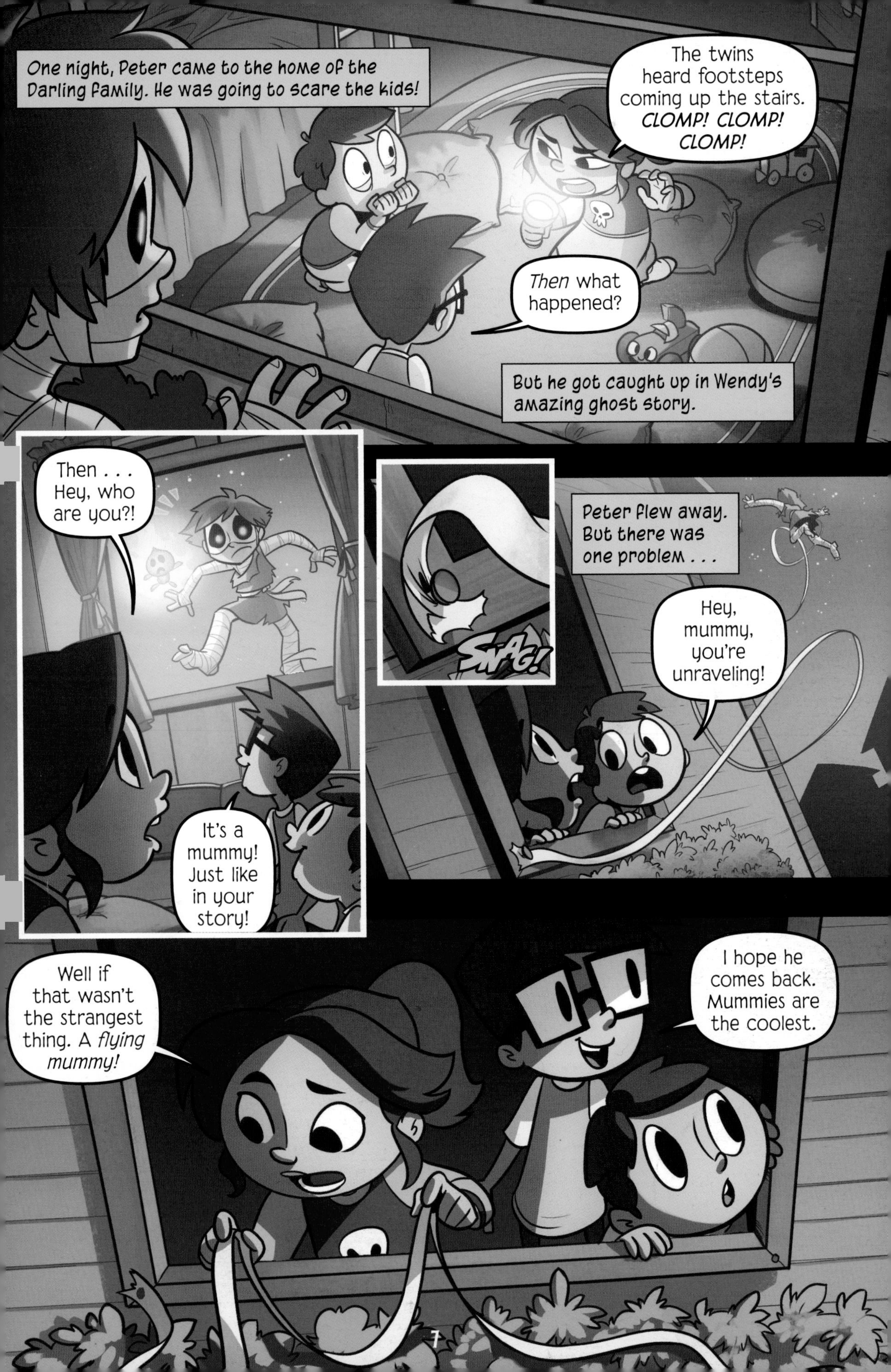
One night, Peter came to the home of the Darling family. He was going to scare the kids!
The twins heard footsteps coming up the stairs. CLOMP! CLOMP! CLOMP!
Then what happened?
But he got caught up in Wendy's amazing ghost story.
Then . . . Hey, who are you?!
It's a mummy! Just like in your story!
SNAG!
Peter flew away. But there was one problem . . .
Hey, mummy, you're unraveling!
Well if that wasn't the strangest thing. A flying mummy!
I hope he comes back. Mummies are the coolest.

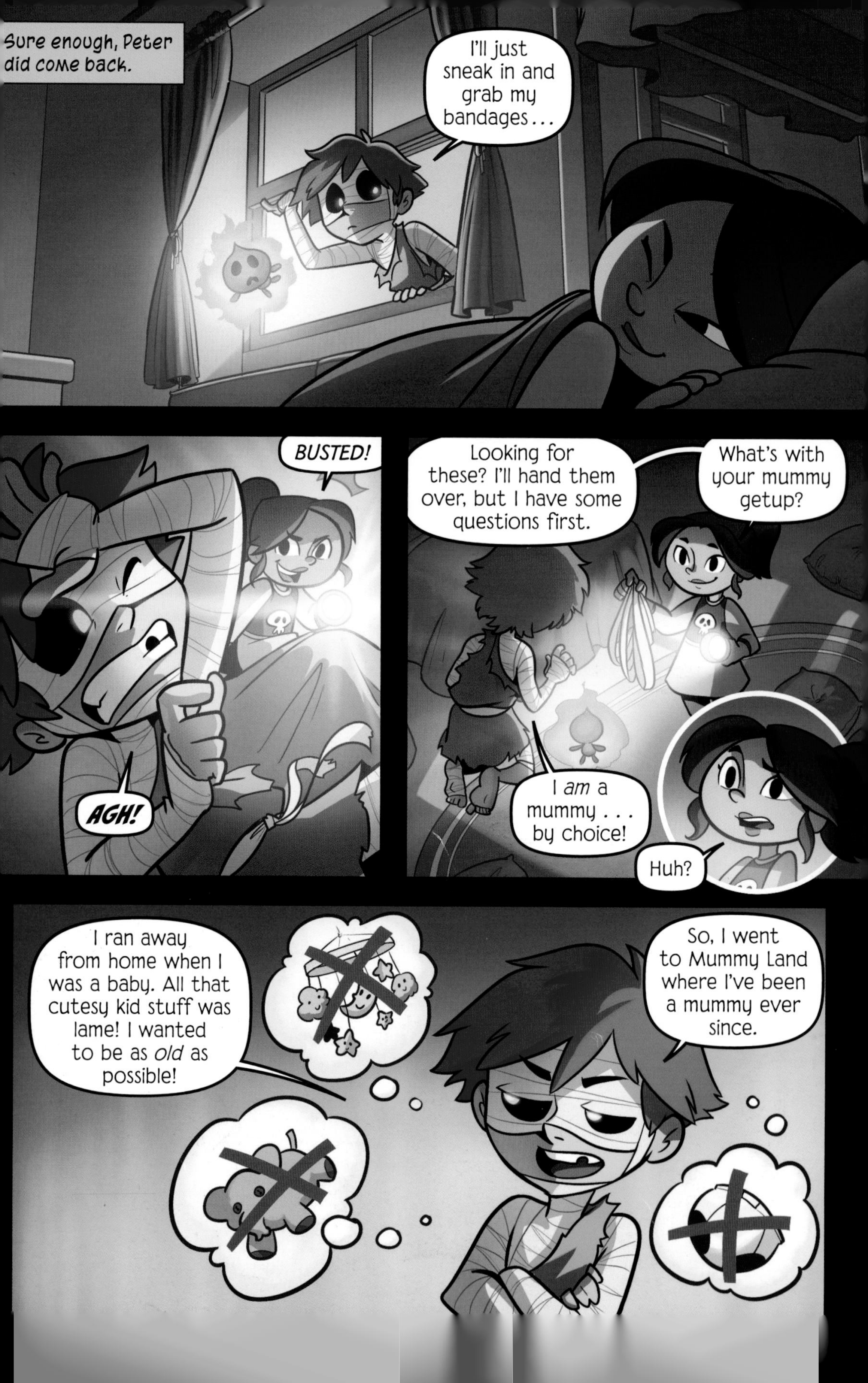

Sure enough, Peter did come back.
I'll just sneak in and grab my bandages . . .
BUSTED!
AGH!
Looking for these? I'll hand them over, but I have some questions first.
What's with your mummy getup?
I *am* a mummy . . . by choice!
Huh?
I ran away from home when I was a baby. All that cutesy kid stuff was lame! I wanted to be as *old* as possible!
So, I went to Mummy Land where I've been a mummy ever since.

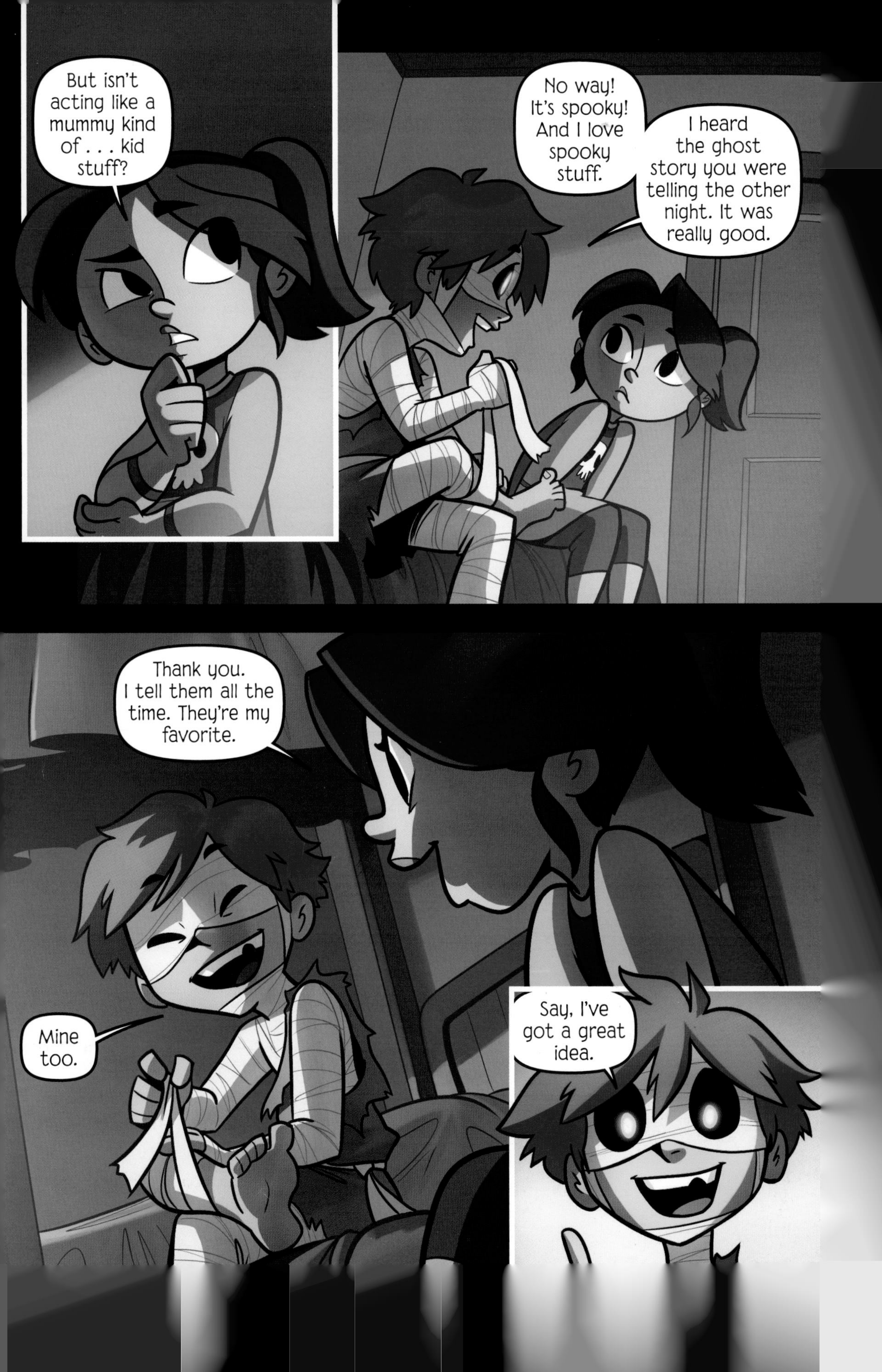
But isn't acting like a mummy kind of . . . kid stuff?
No way! It's spooky! And I love spooky stuff.
I heard the ghost story you were telling the other night. It was really good.
Thank you. I tell them all the time. They're my favorite.
Mine too.
Say, I've got a great idea.

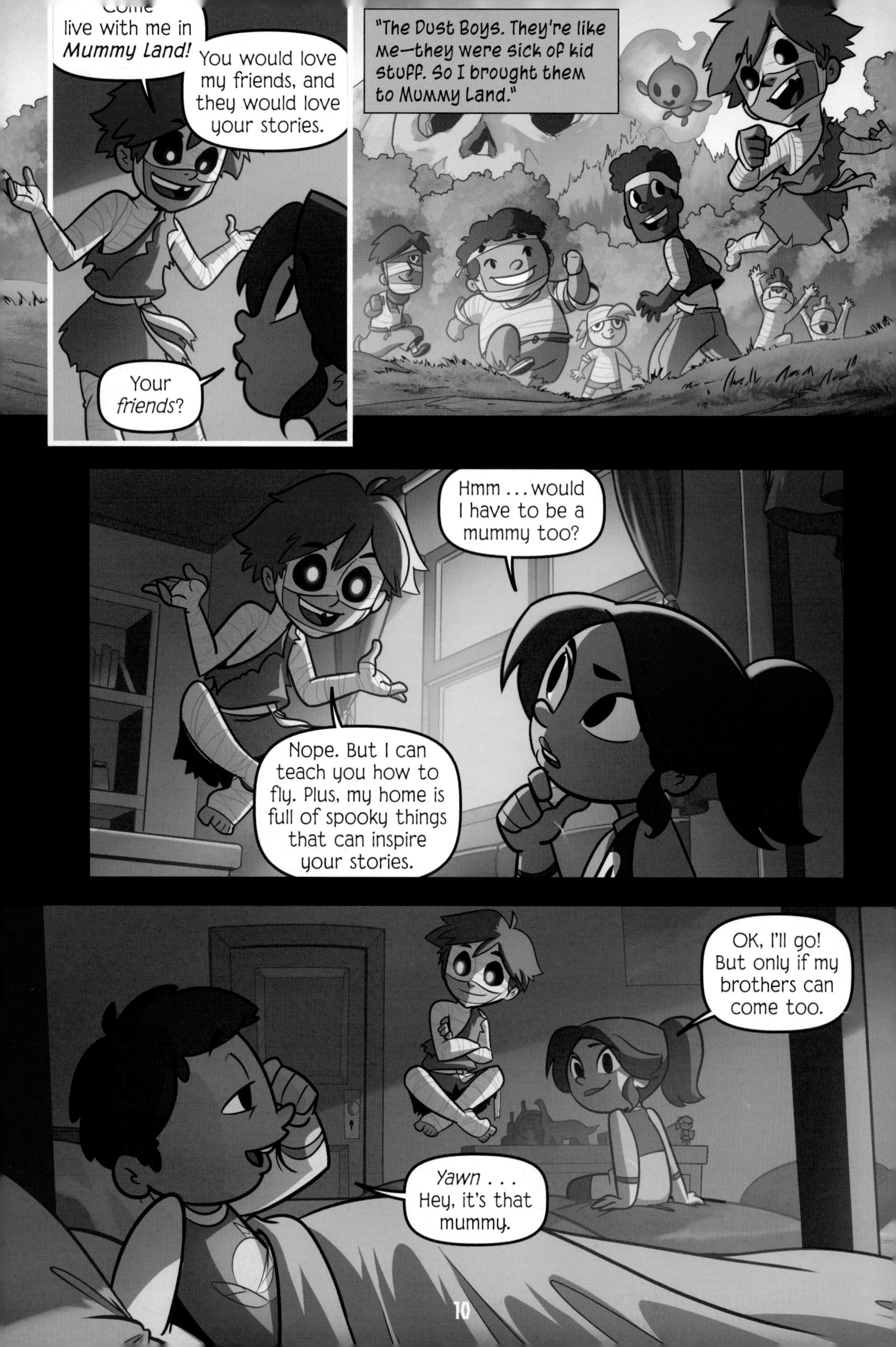
Come live with me in Mummy Land!
You would love my friends, and they would love your stories.
Your friends?
"The Dust Boys. They're like me—they were sick of kid stuff. So I brought them to Mummy Land."
Hmm . . . would I have to be a mummy too?
Nope. But I can teach you how to fly. Plus, my home is full of spooky things that can inspire your stories.
OK, I'll go! But only if my brothers can come too.
Yawn . . . Hey, it's that mummy.

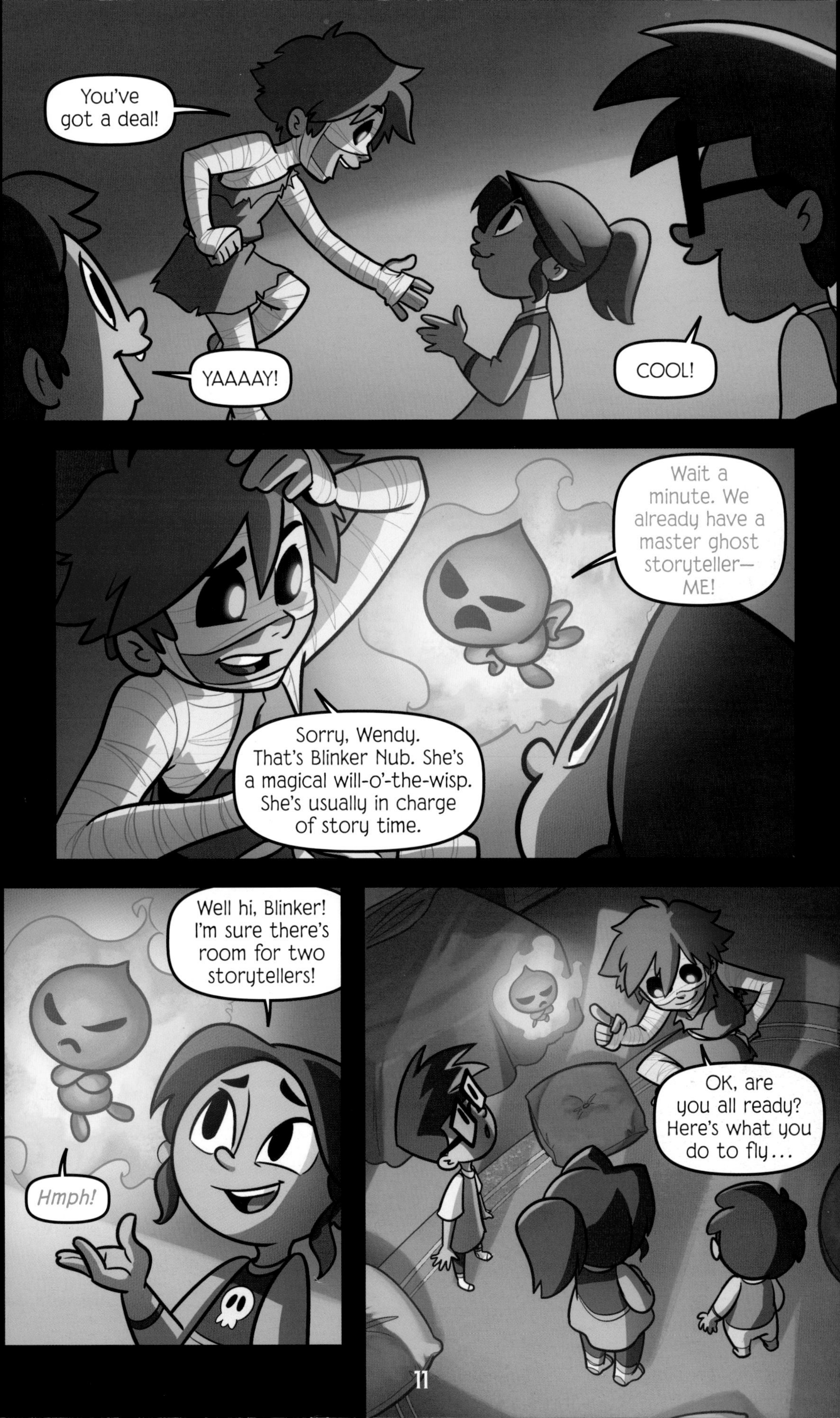
You've got a deal!
YAAAAY!
COOL!
Wait a minute. We already have a master ghost storyteller—ME!
Sorry, Wendy. That's Blinker Nub. She's a magical will-o'-the-wisp. She's usually in charge of story time.
Well hi, Blinker! I'm sure there's room for two storytellers!
Hmph!
OK, are you all ready? Here's what you do to fly...

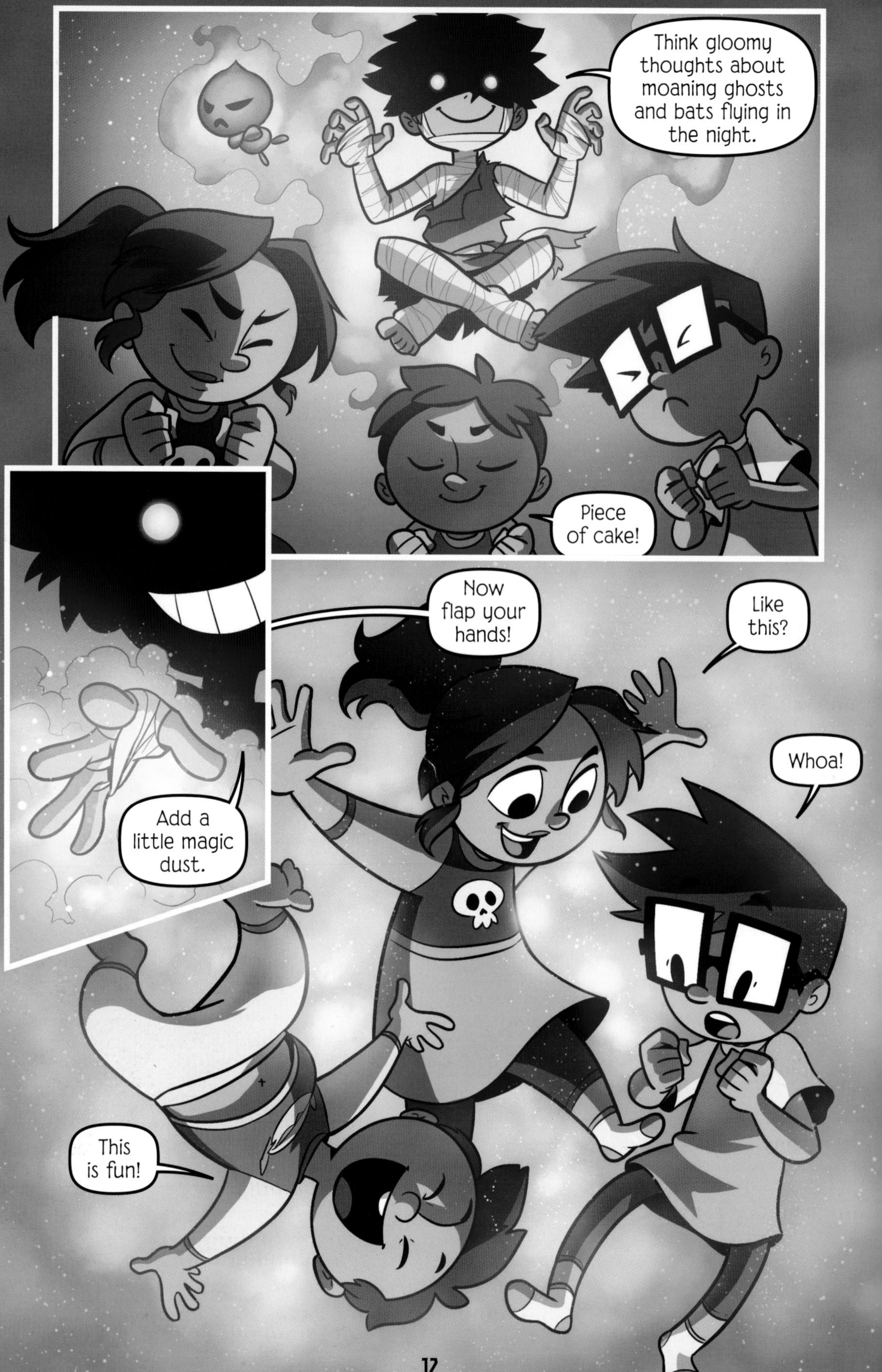

Think gloomy thoughts about moaning ghosts and bats flying in the night.
Piece of cake!
Now flap your hands!
Like this?
Add a little magic dust.
Whoa!
This is fun!

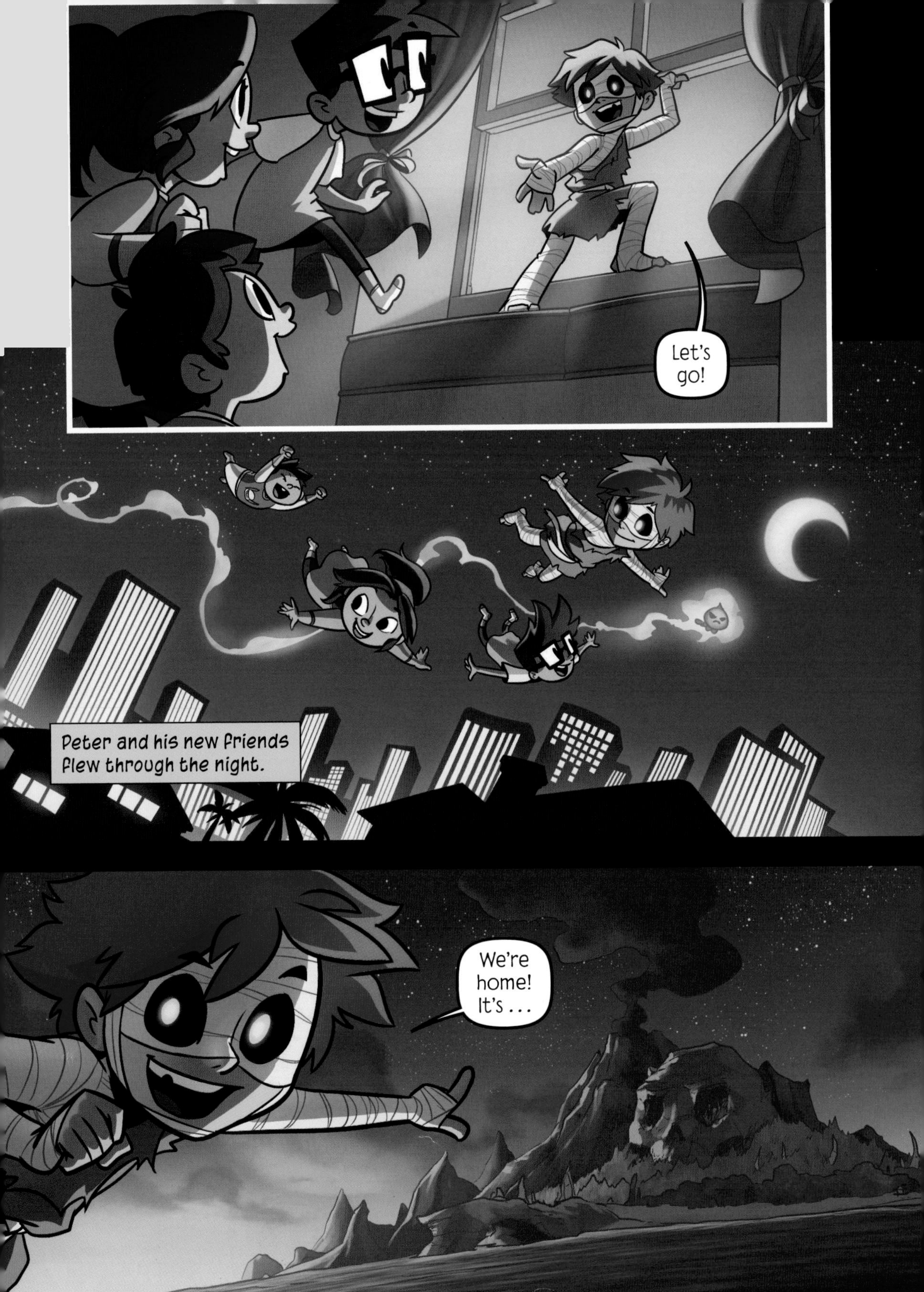
Let's go!
Peter and his new friends flew through the night.
We're home! It's . . .

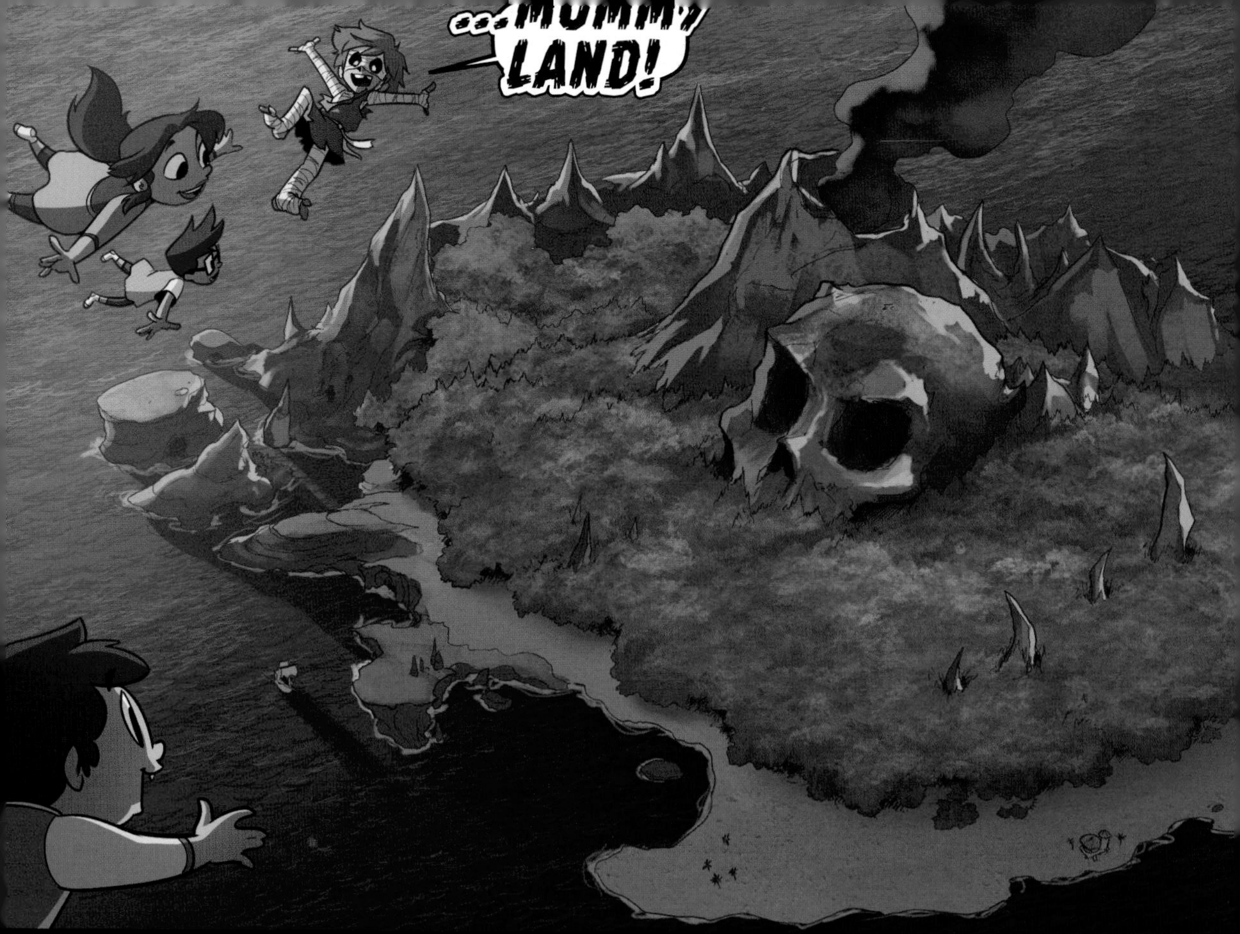
...MUMMY LAND!

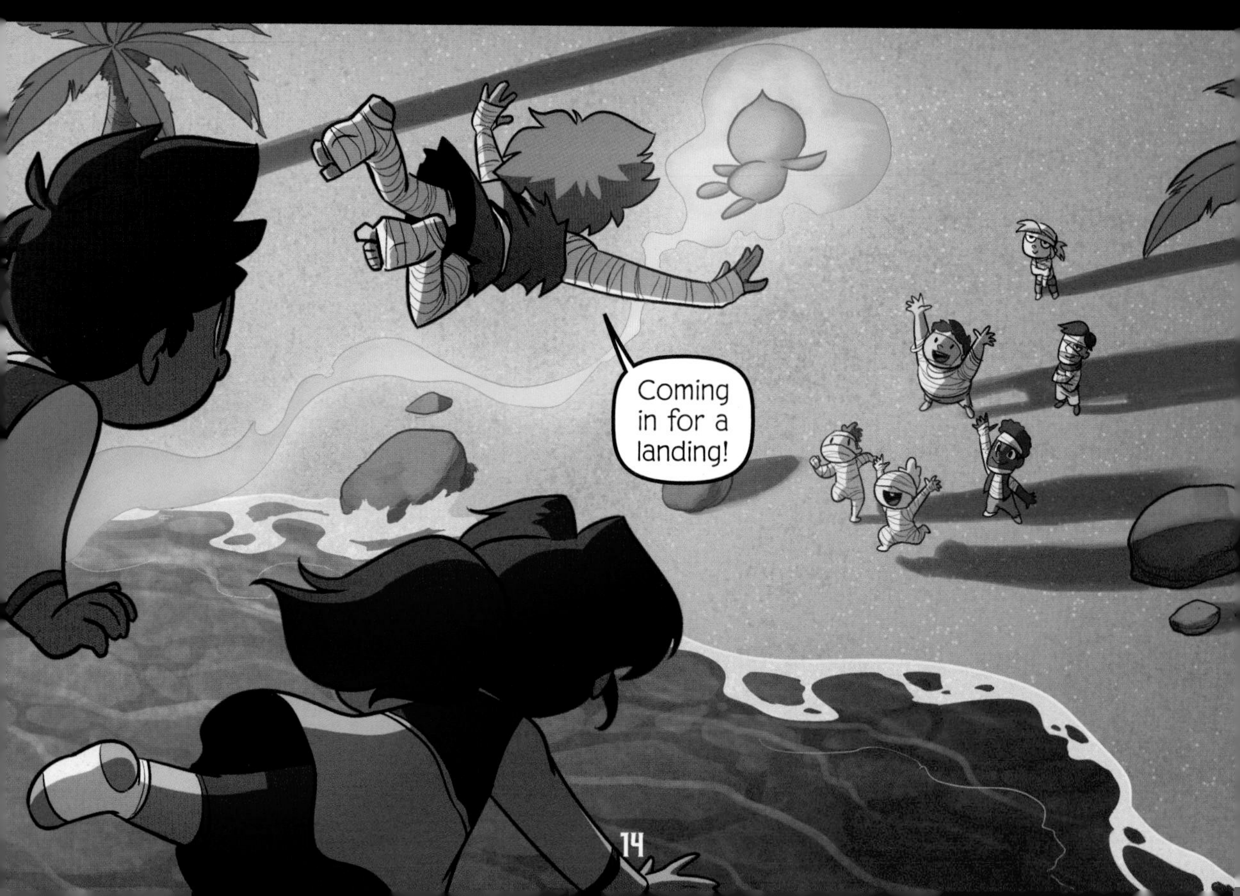
Coming in for a landing!

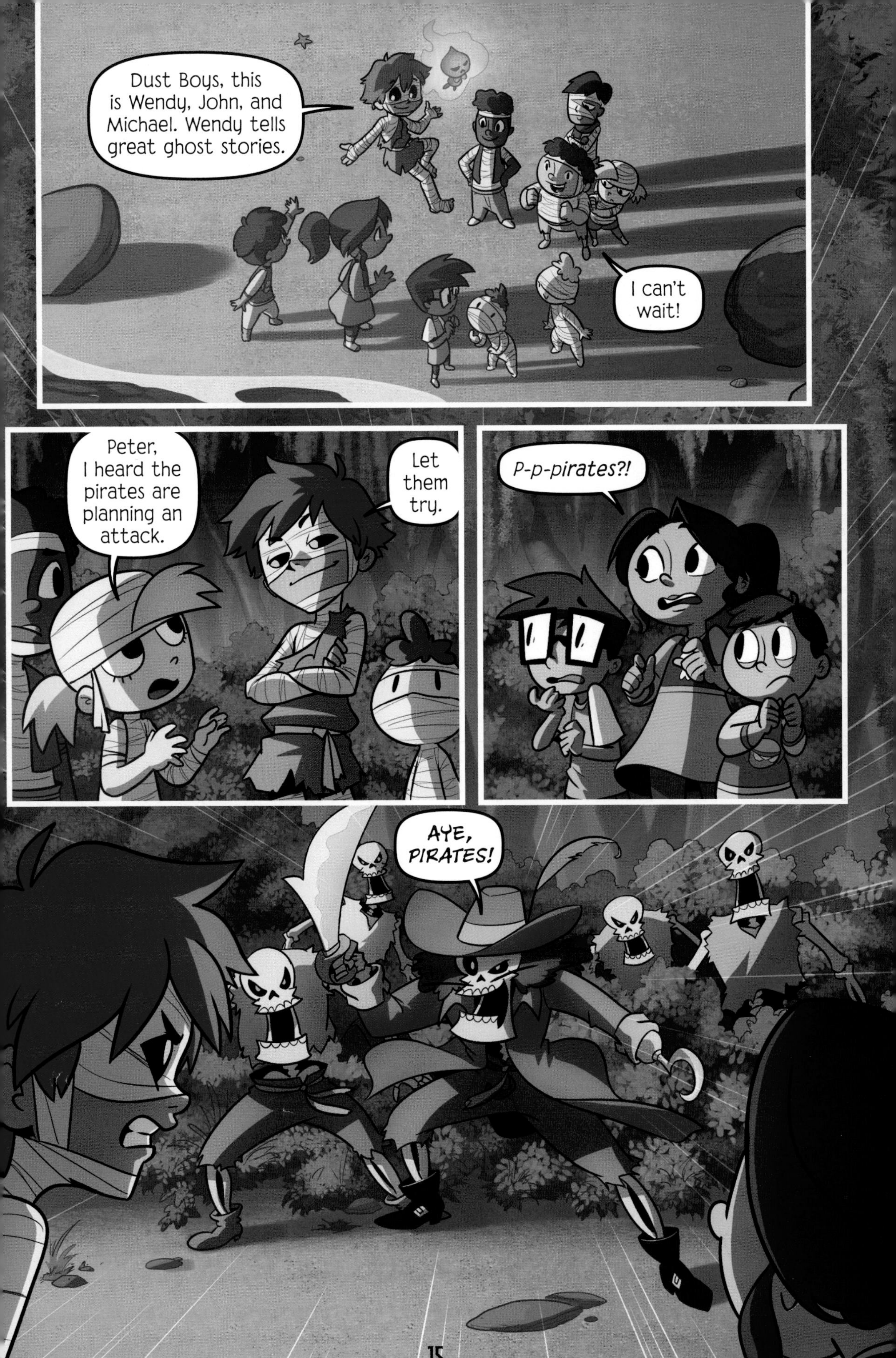
Dust Boys, this is Wendy, John, and Michael. Wendy tells great ghost stories.
I can't wait!
Peter, I heard the pirates are planning an attack.
Let them try.
P-p-pirates?!
AYE, PIRATES!

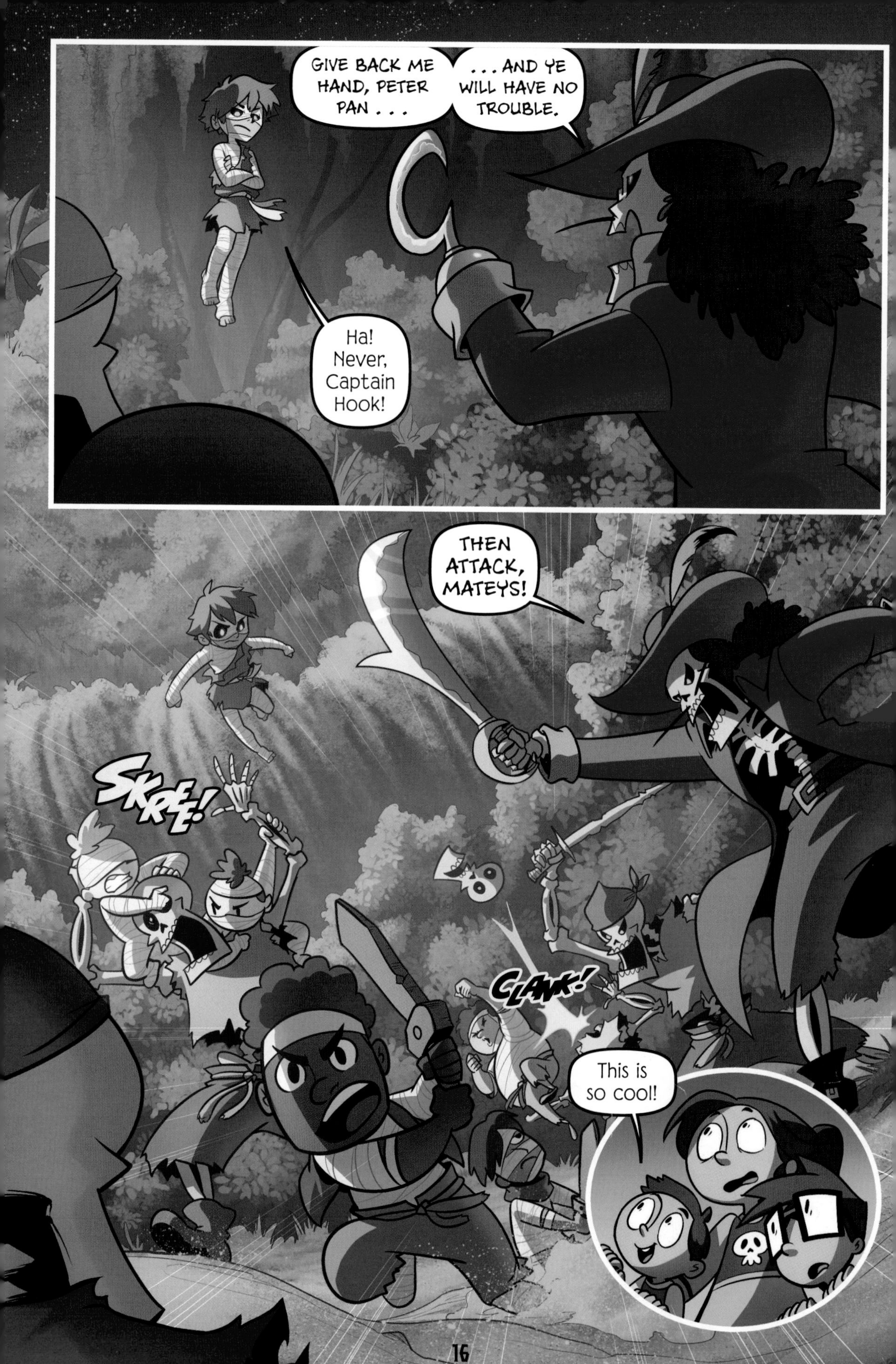
GIVE BACK ME HAND, PETER PAN . . .
. . . AND YE WILL HAVE NO TROUBLE.
Ha! Never, Captain Hook!
THEN ATTACK, MATEYS!
SKREE!
CLANK!
This is so cool!

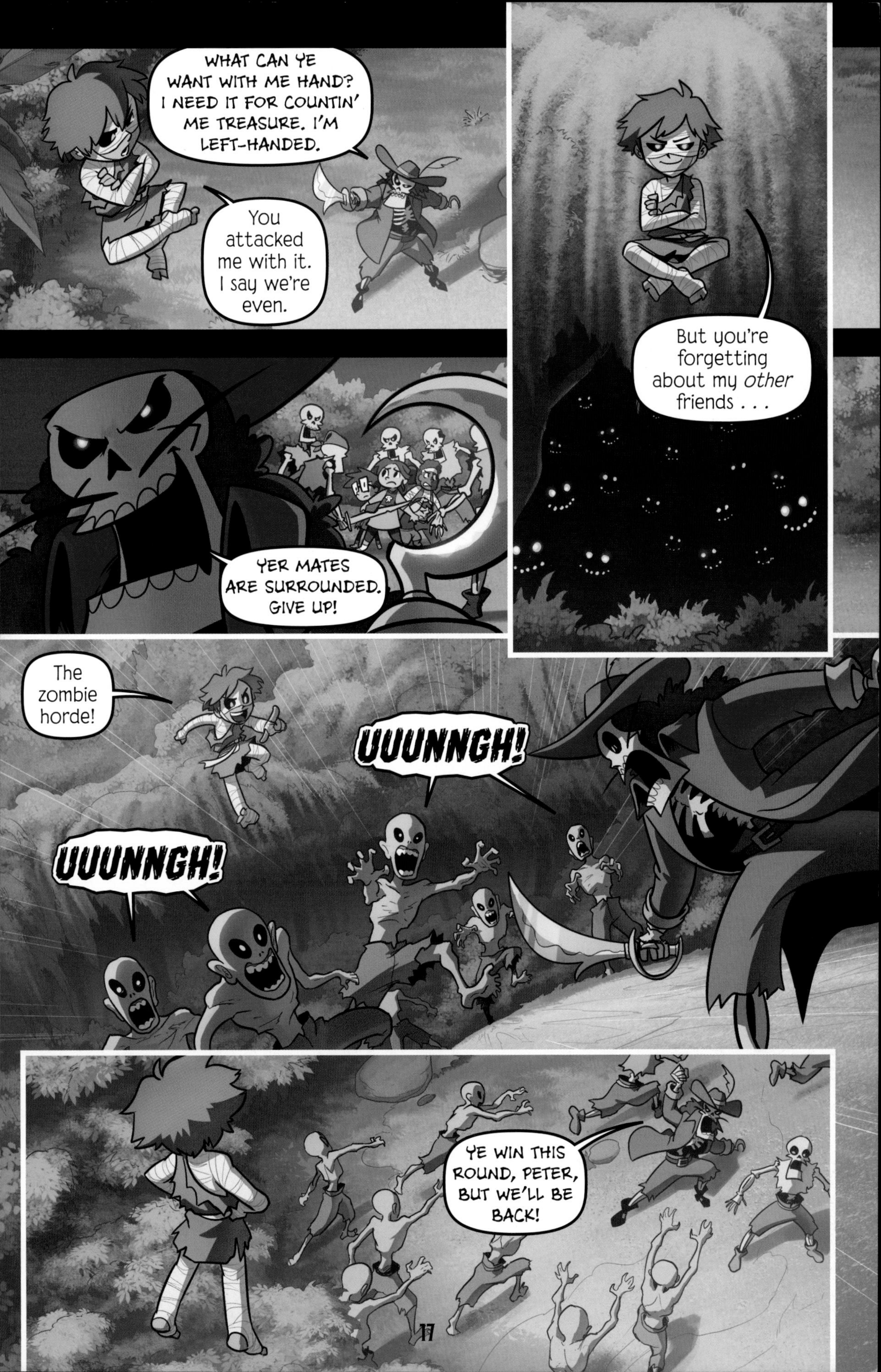
WHAT CAN YE WANT WITH ME HAND? I NEED IT FOR COUNTIN' ME TREASURE. I'M LEFT-HANDED.
You attacked me with it. I say we're even.
But you're forgetting about my *other* friends . . .
YER MATES ARE SURROUNDED. GIVE UP!
The zombie horde!
UUUNNGH!
UUUNNGH!
YE WIN THIS ROUND, PETER, BUT WE'LL BE BACK!

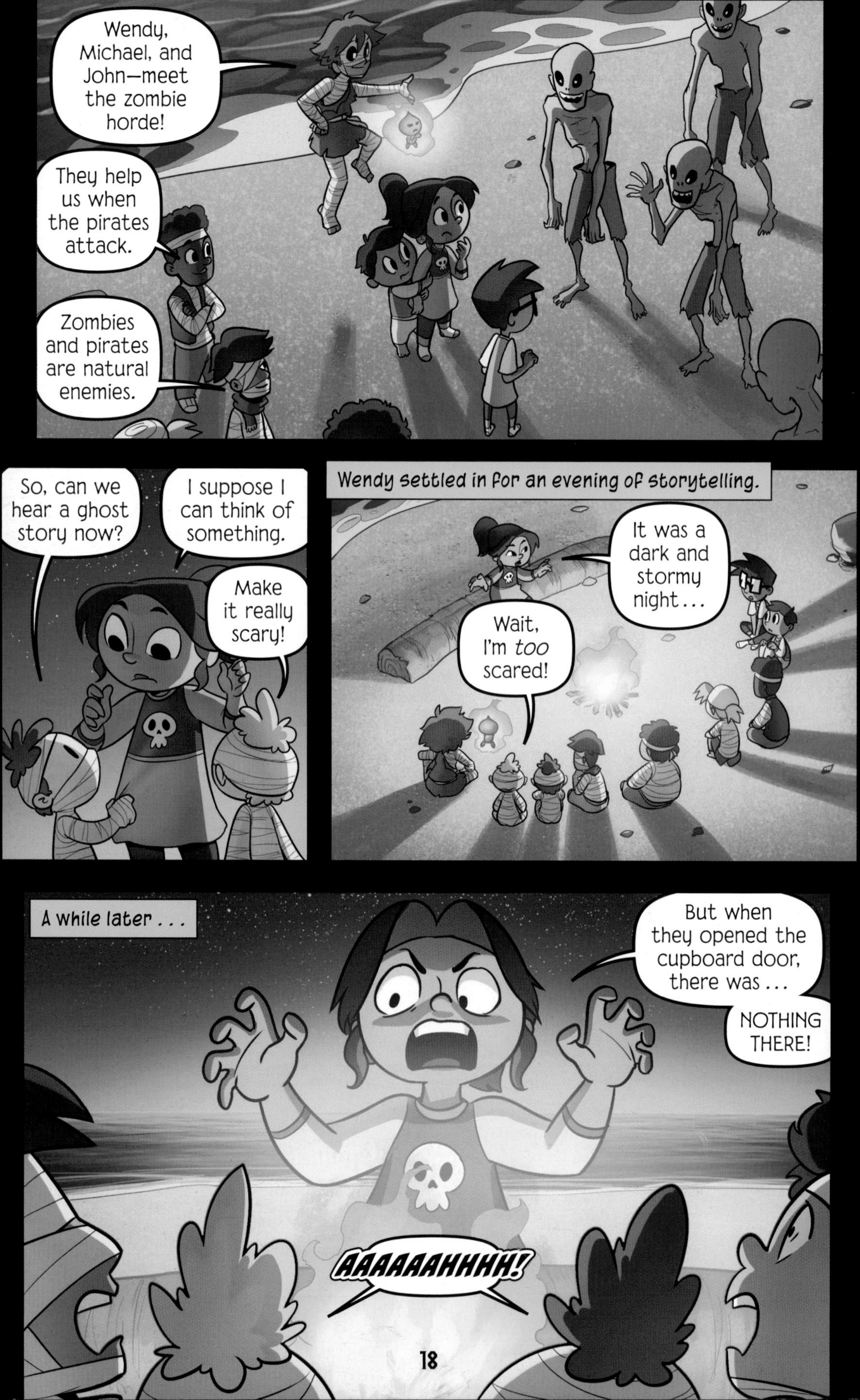
Wendy, Michael, and John—meet the zombie horde!
They help us when the pirates attack.
Zombies and pirates are natural enemies.
So, can we hear a ghost story now?
I suppose I can think of something.
Make it really scary!
Wendy settled in for an evening of storytelling.
It was a dark and stormy night . . .
Wait, I'm *too* scared!
A while later . . .
But when they opened the cupboard door, there was . . .
NOTHING THERE!
AAAAAAHHHH!

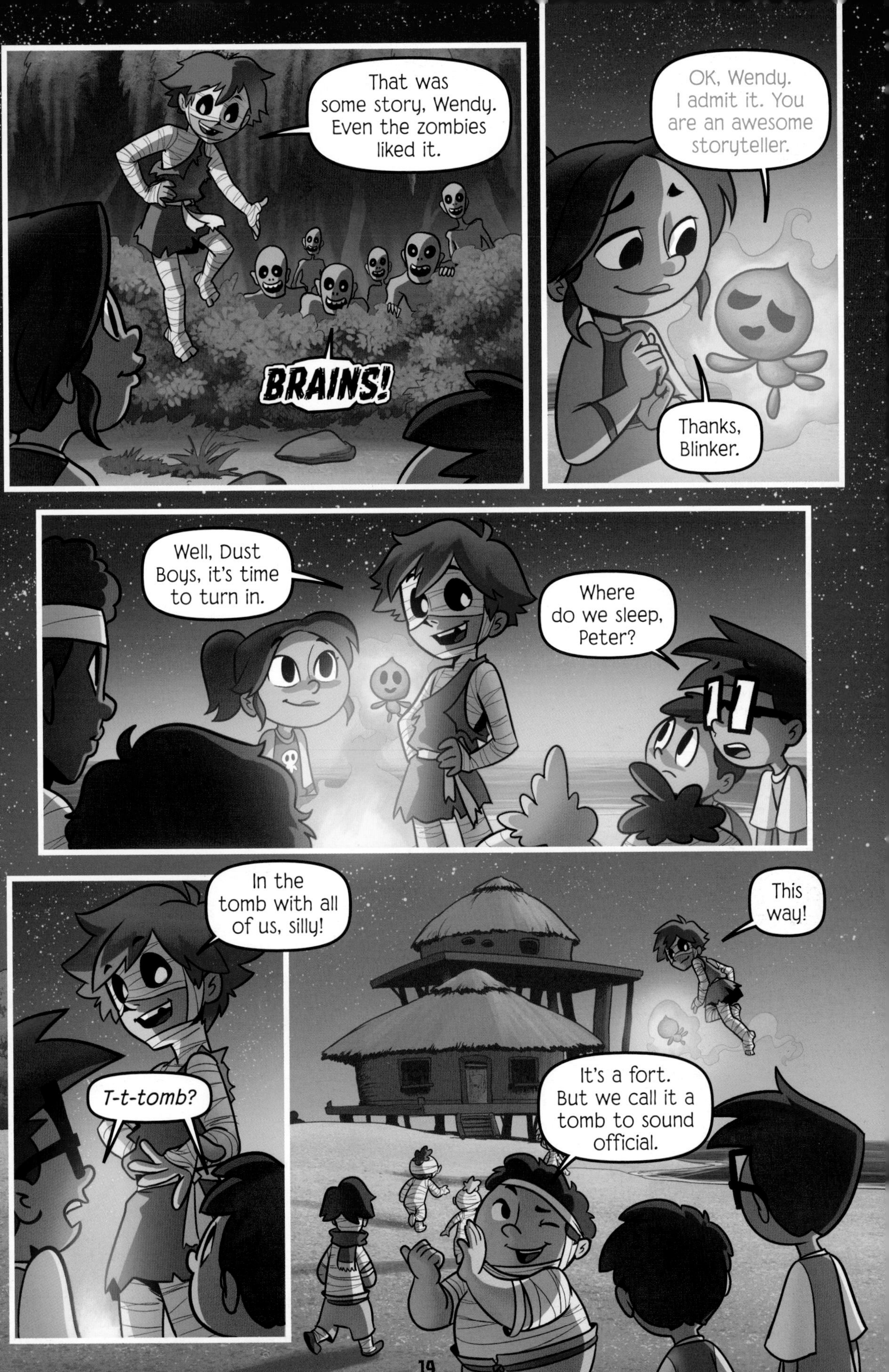
That was some story, Wendy. Even the zombies liked it.
BRAINS!
OK, Wendy. I admit it. You are an awesome storyteller.
Thanks, Blinker.
Well, Dust Boys, it's time to turn in.
Where do we sleep, Peter?
In the tomb with all of us, silly!
T-t-tomb?
This way!
It's a fort. But we call it a tomb to sound official.

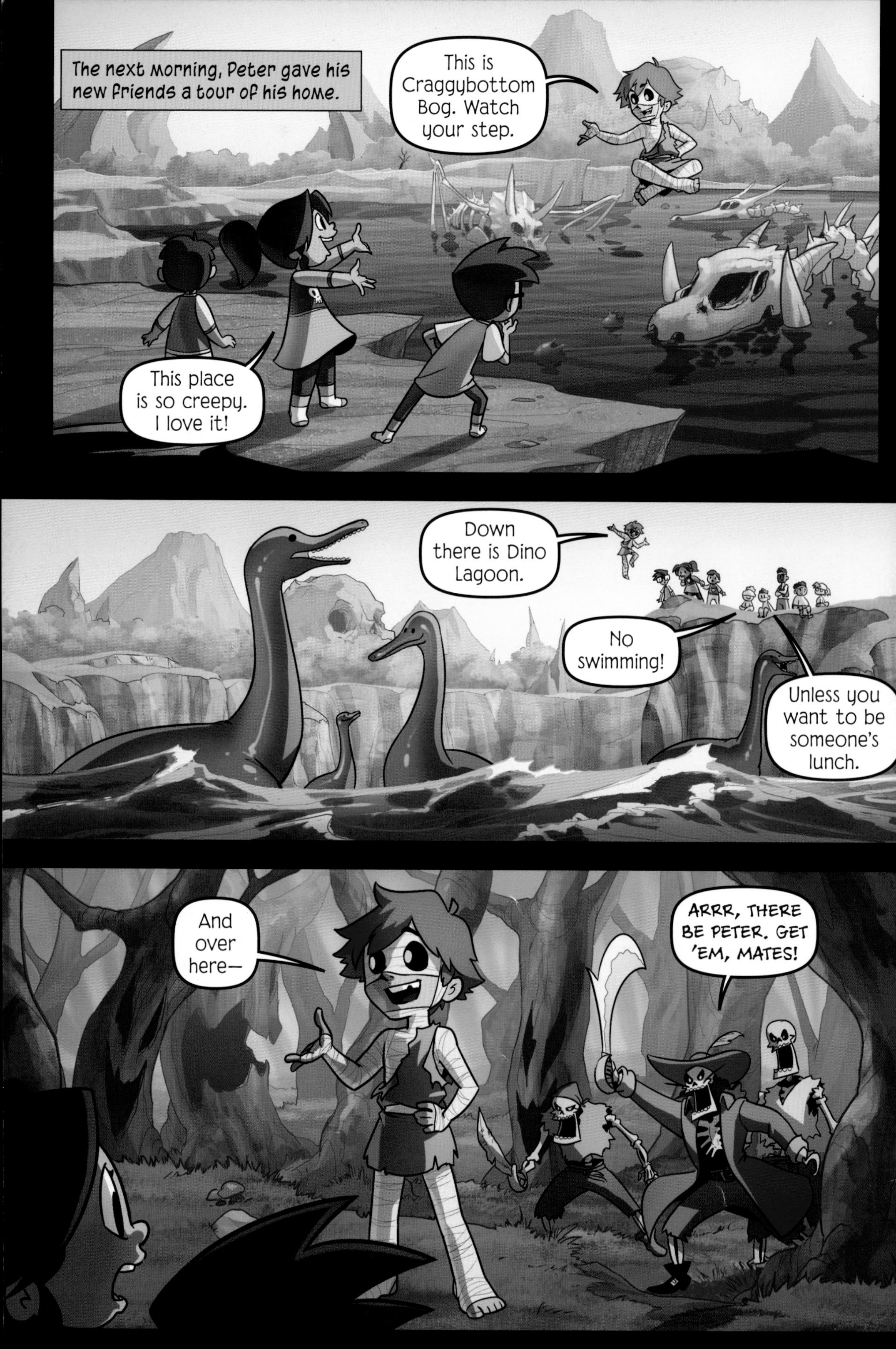
The next morning, Peter gave his new friends a tour of his home.
This is Craggybottom Bog. Watch your step.
This place is so creepy. I love it!
Down there is Dino Lagoon.
No swimming!
Unless you want to be someone's lunch.
And over here—
ARRR, THERE BE PETER. GET 'EM, MATES!

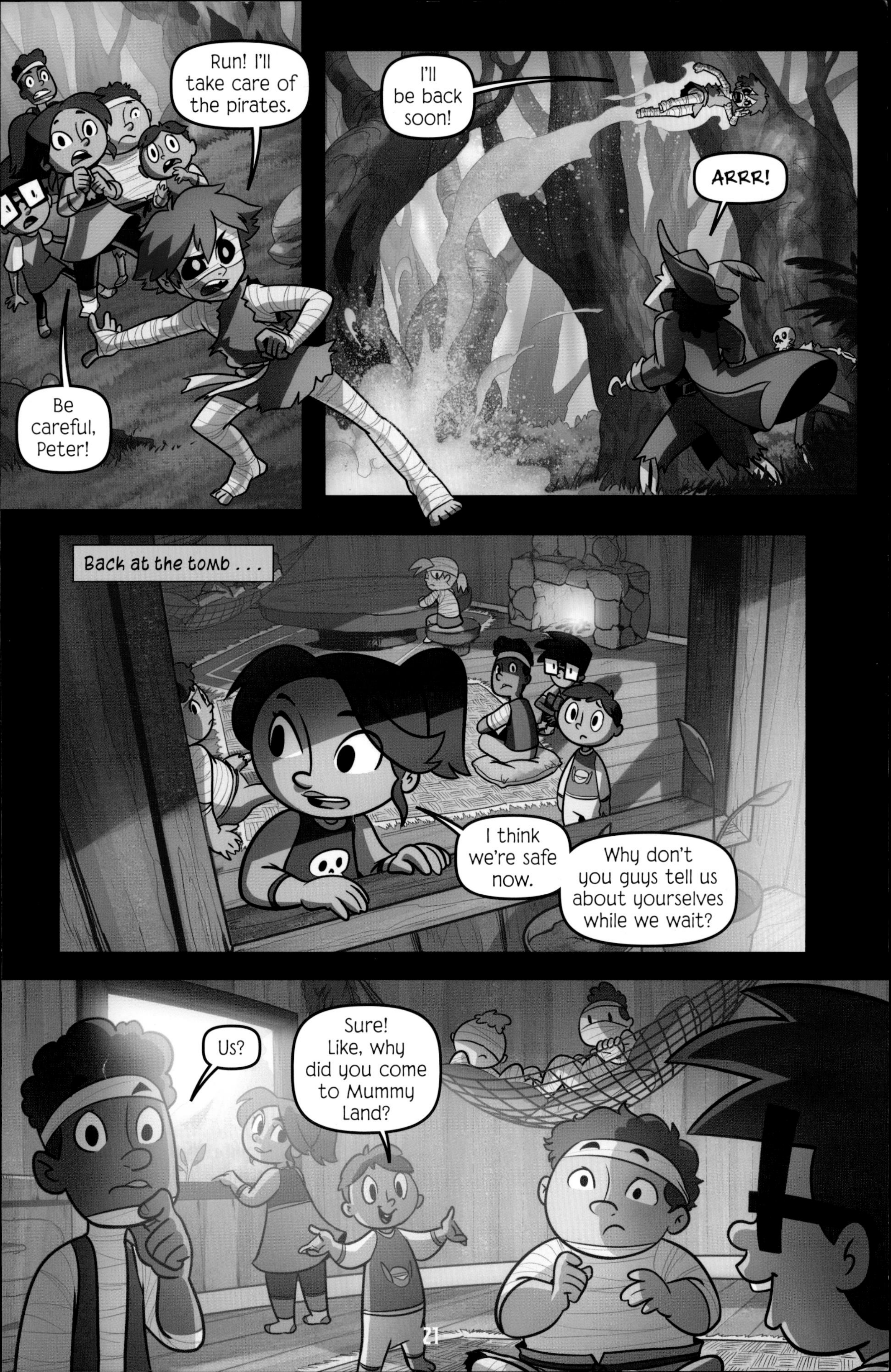

Run! I'll take care of the pirates.
Be careful, Peter!
I'll be back soon!
ARRR!
Back at the tomb . . .
I think we're safe now.
Why don't you guys tell us about yourselves while we wait?
Us?
Sure! Like, why did you come to Mummy Land?

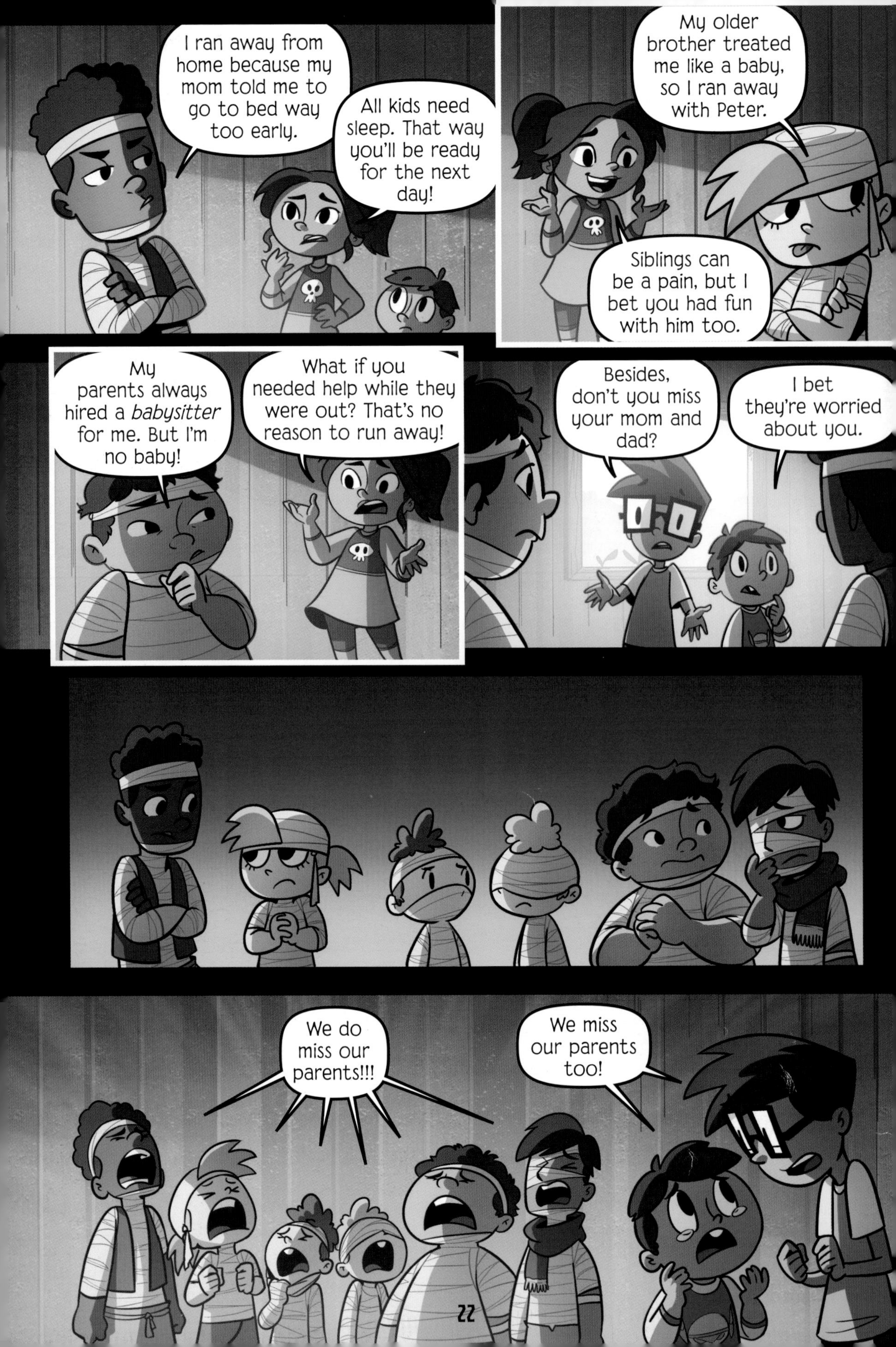
I ran away from home because my mom told me to go to bed way too early.
All kids need sleep. That way you'll be ready for the next day!
My older brother treated me like a baby, so I ran away with Peter.
Siblings can be a pain, but I bet you had fun with him too.
My parents always hired a *babysitter* for me. But I'm no baby!
What if you needed help while they were out? That's no reason to run away!
Besides, don't you miss your mom and dad?
I bet they're worried about you.
We do miss our parents!!!
We miss our parents too!

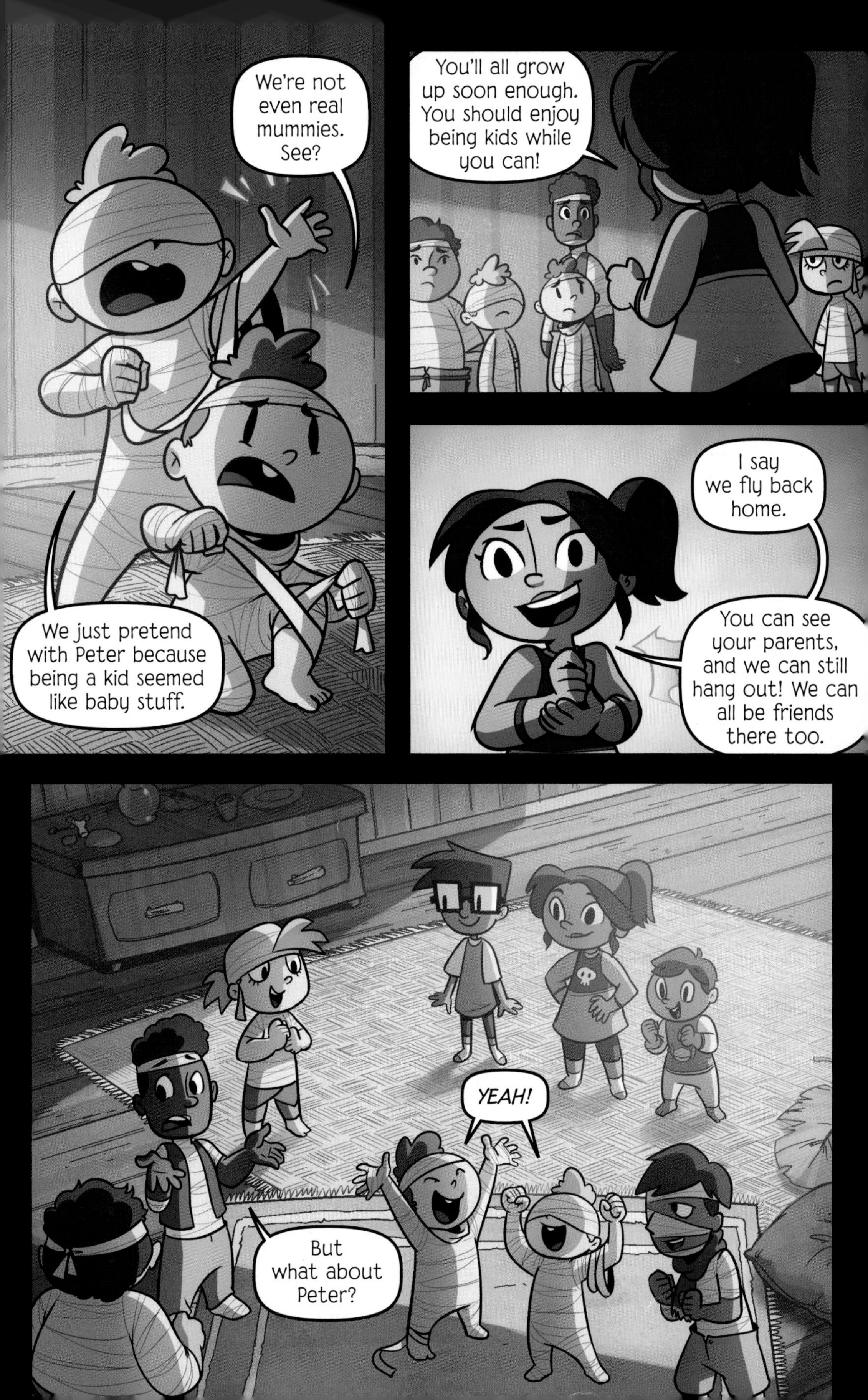
We're not even real mummies. See?
We just pretend with Peter because being a kid seemed like baby stuff.
You'll all grow up soon enough. You should enjoy being kids while you can!
I say we fly back home.
You can see your parents, and we can still hang out! We can all be friends there too.
YEAH!
But what about Peter?

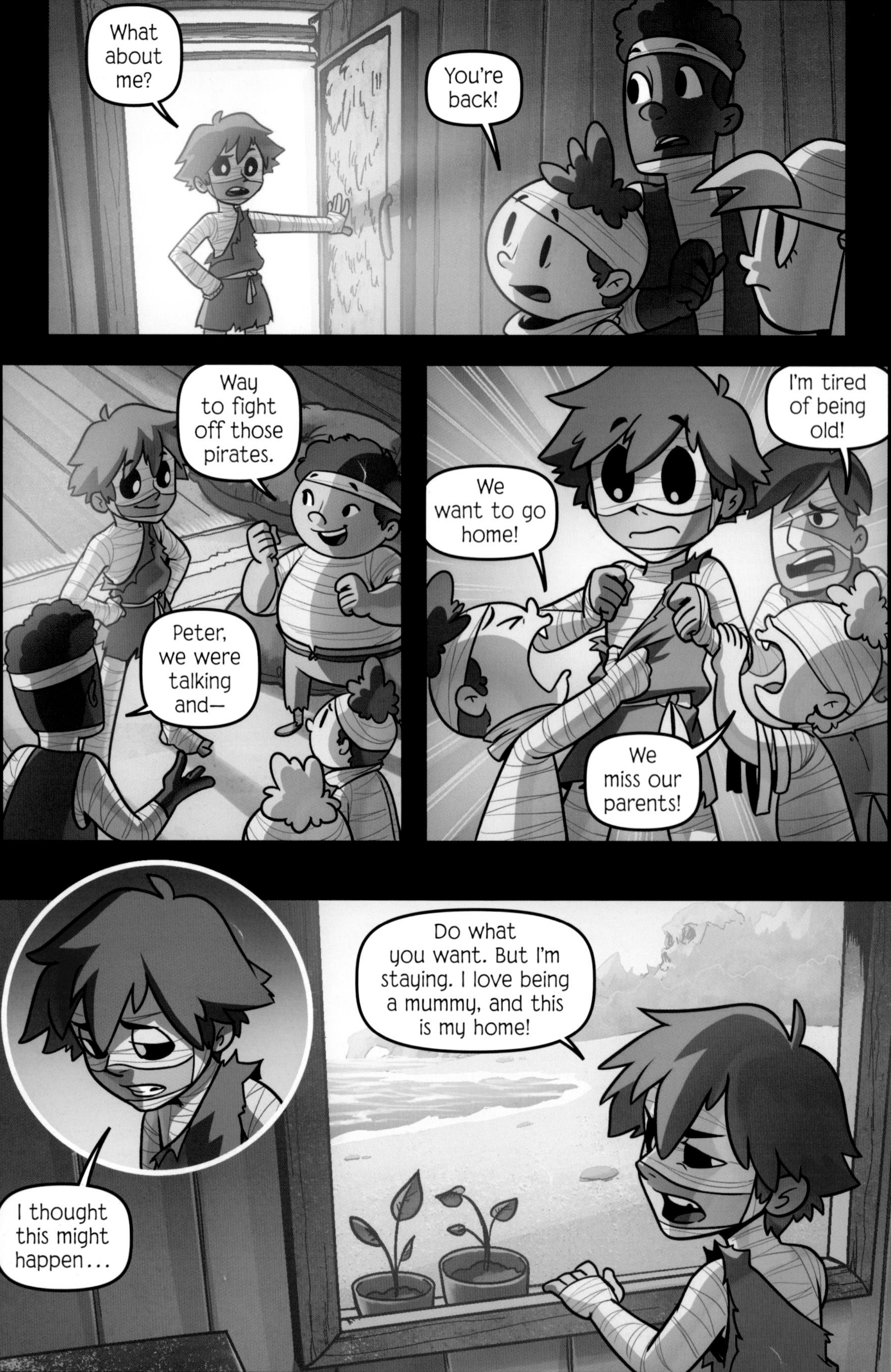
What about me?
You're back!
Way to fight off those pirates.
Peter, we were talking and—
We want to go home!
I'm tired of being old!
We miss our parents!
I thought this might happen...
Do what you want. But I'm staying. I love being a mummy, and this is my home!

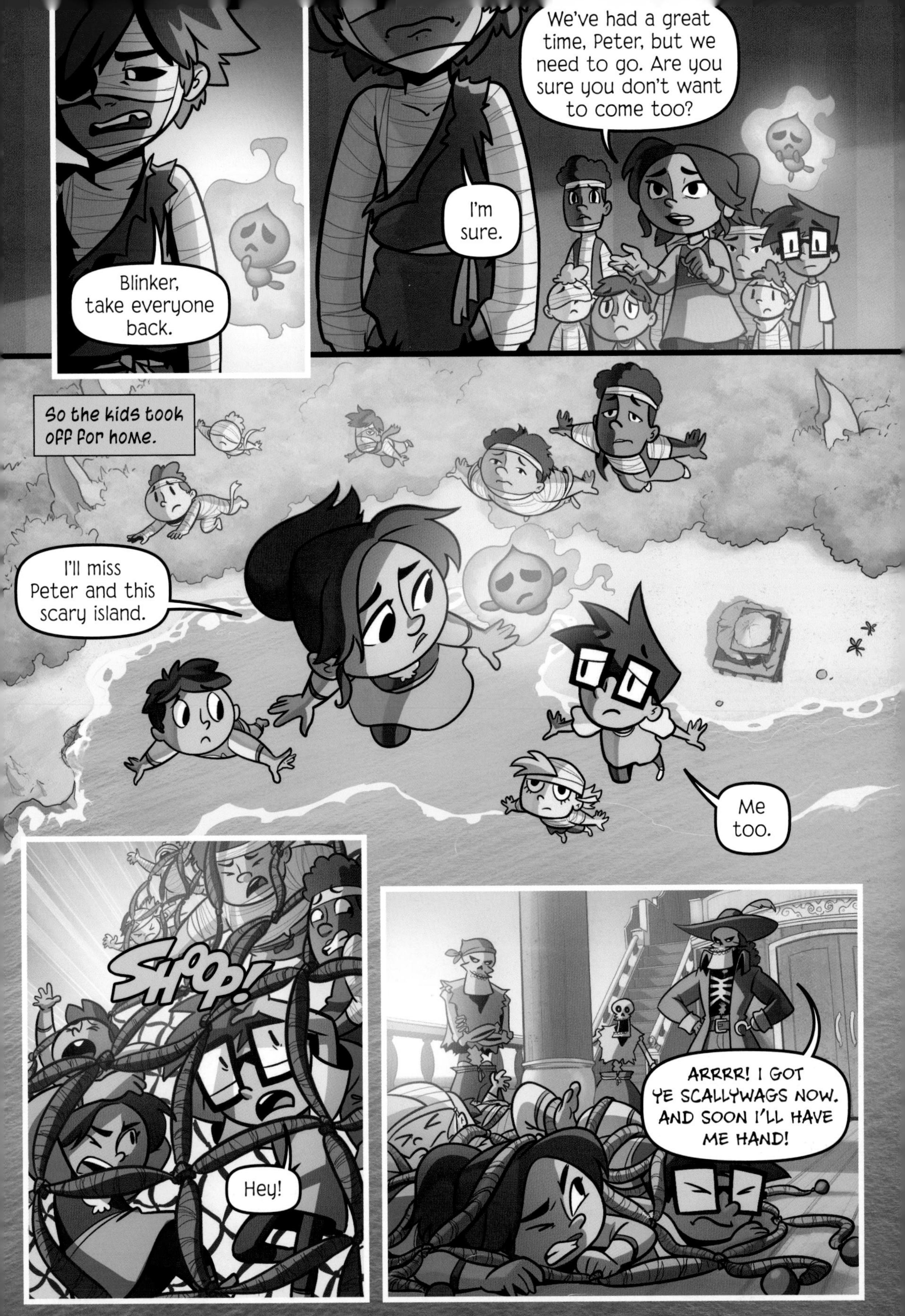
We've had a great time, Peter, but we need to go. Are you sure you don't want to come too?
I'm sure.
Blinker, take everyone back.
So the kids took off for home.
I'll miss Peter and this scary island.
Me too.
SHOOP!
Hey!
ARRRR! I GOT YE SCALLYWAGS NOW. AND SOON I'LL HAVE ME HAND!

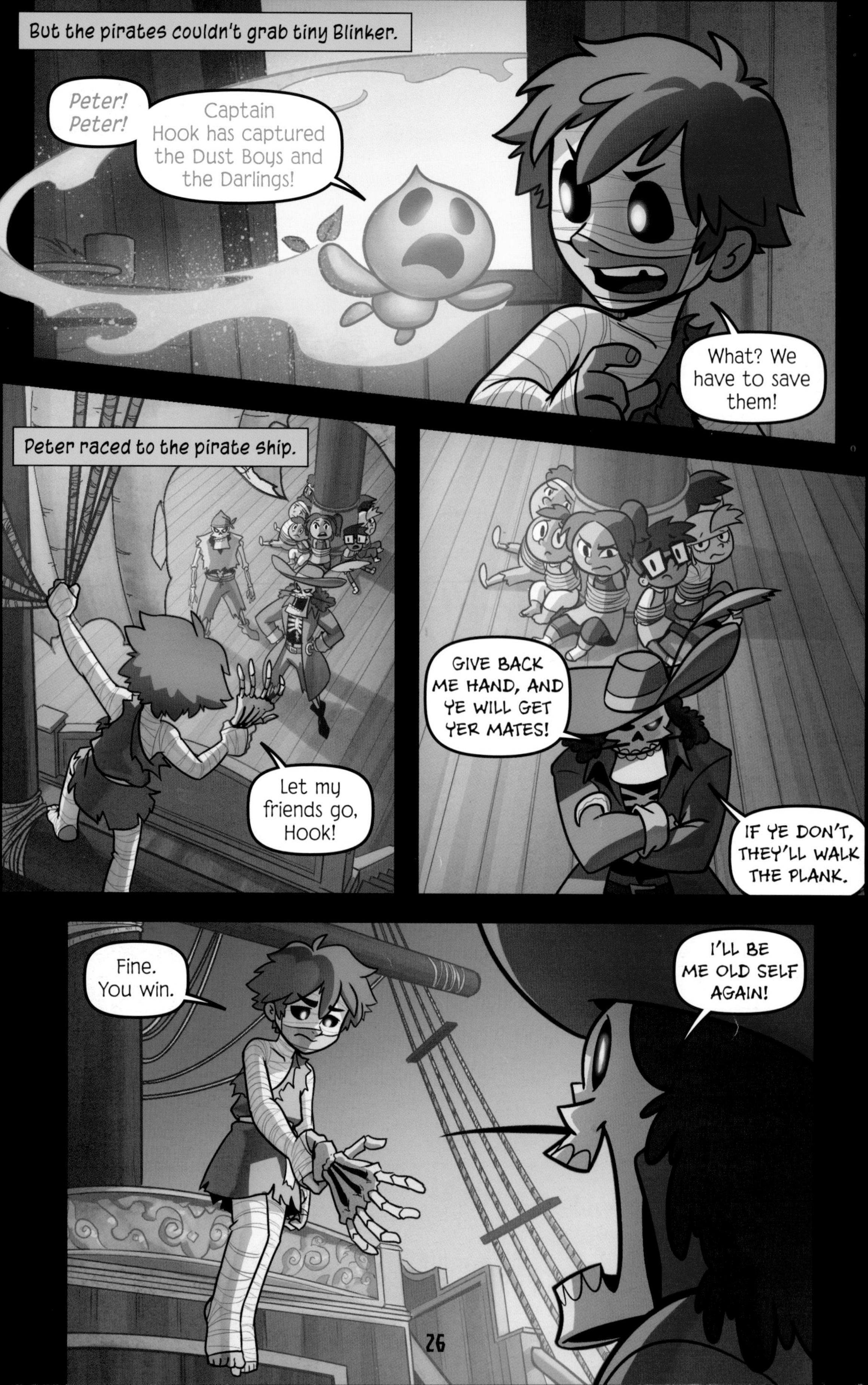
But the pirates couldn't grab tiny Blinker.
Peter! Peter!
Captain Hook has captured the Dust Boys and the Darlings!
What? We have to save them!
Peter raced to the pirate ship.
Let my friends go, Hook!
GIVE BACK ME HAND, AND YE WILL GET YER MATES!
IF YE DON'T, THEY'LL WALK THE PLANK.
Fine. You win.
I'LL BE ME OLD SELF AGAIN!

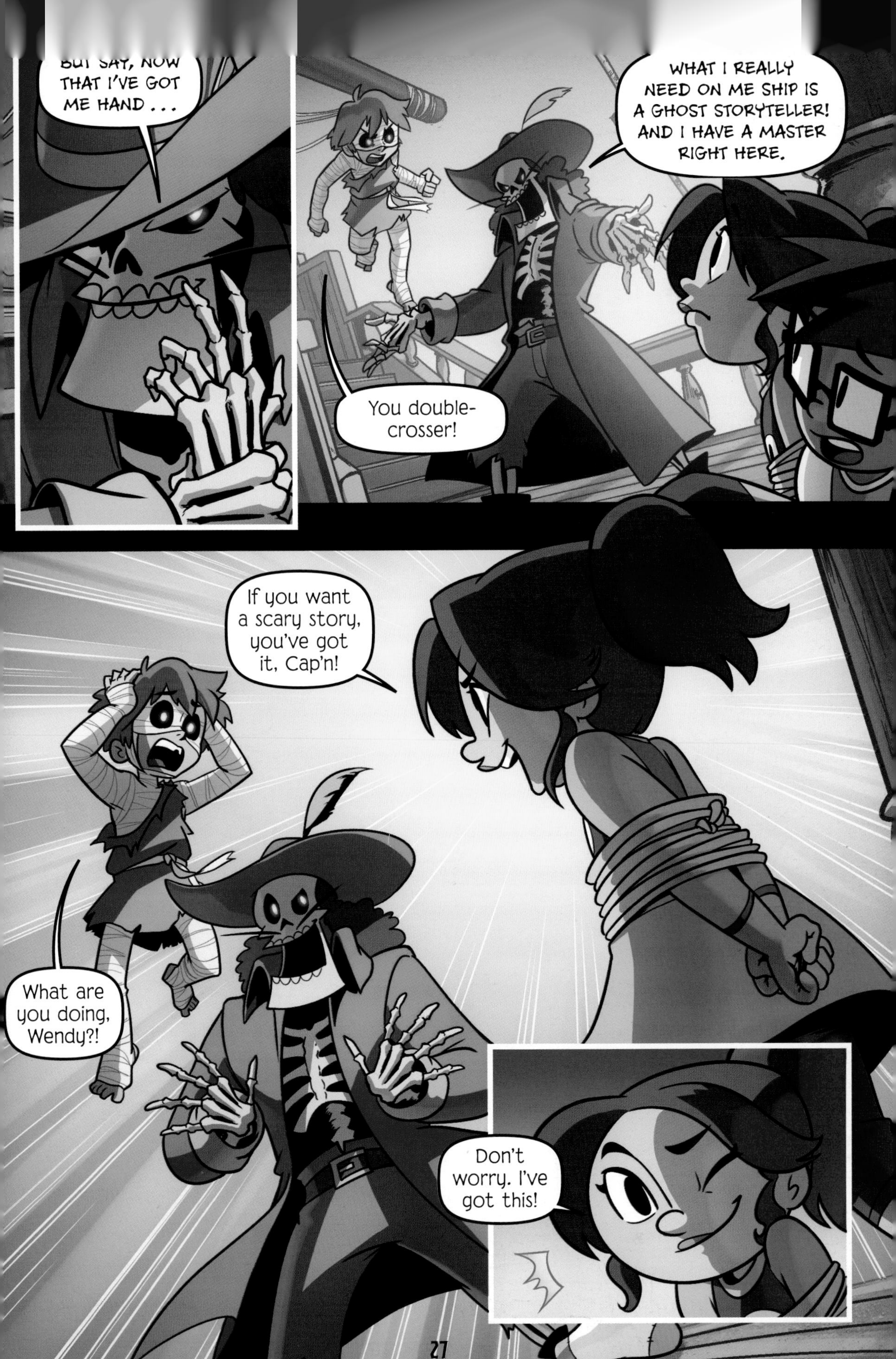
BUT SAY, NOW THAT I'VE GOT ME HAND . . .
WHAT I REALLY NEED ON ME SHIP IS A GHOST STORYTELLER! AND I HAVE A MASTER RIGHT HERE.
You double-crosser!
If you want a scary story, you've got it, Cap'n!
What are you doing, Wendy?!
Don't worry. I've got this!

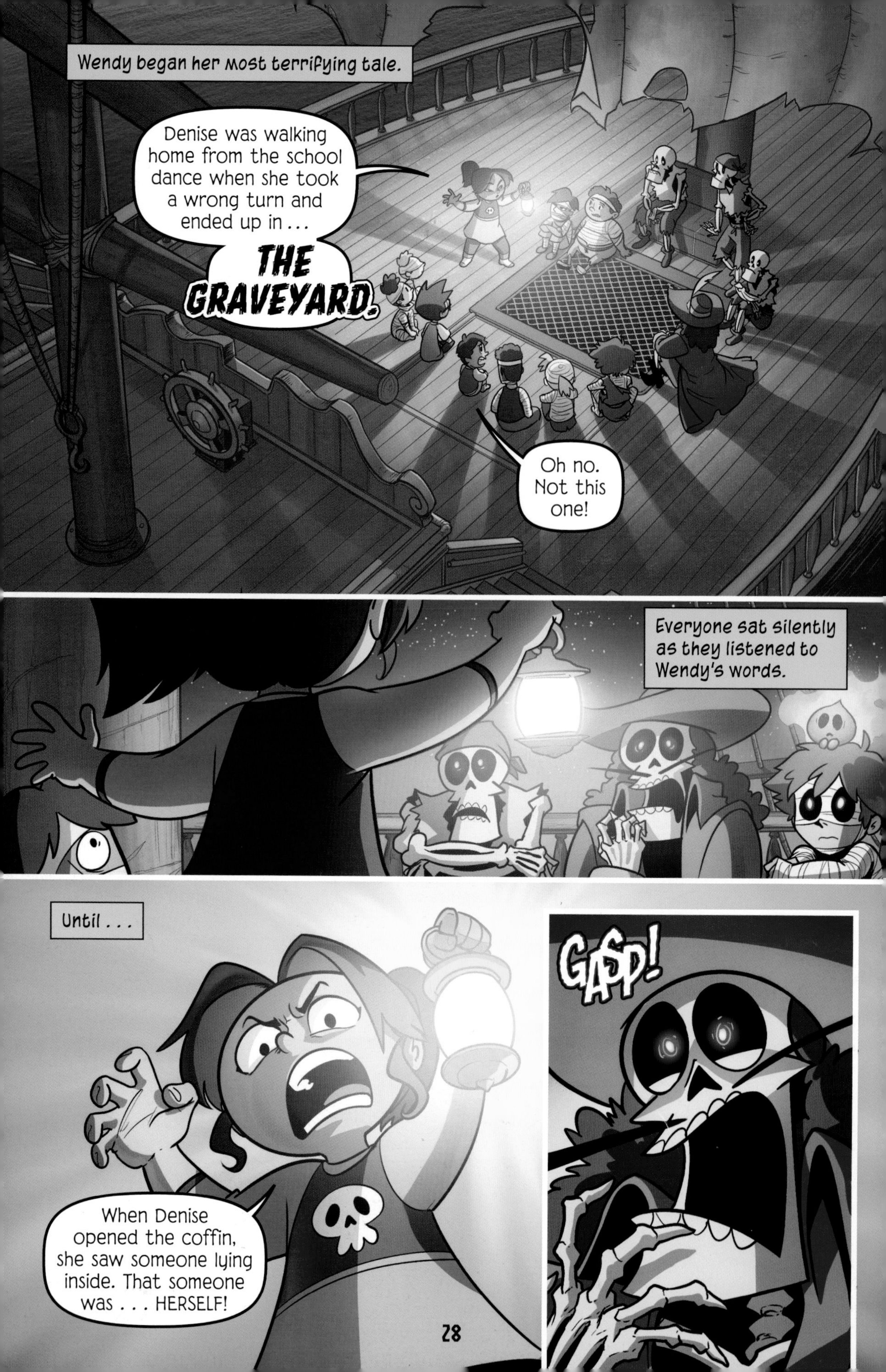
Wendy began her most terrifying tale.
Denise was walking home from the school dance when she took a wrong turn and ended up in . . .
THE GRAVEYARD.
Oh no. Not this one!
Everyone sat silently as they listened to Wendy's words.
Until . . .
When Denise opened the coffin, she saw someone lying inside. That someone was . . . HERSELF!
GASP!

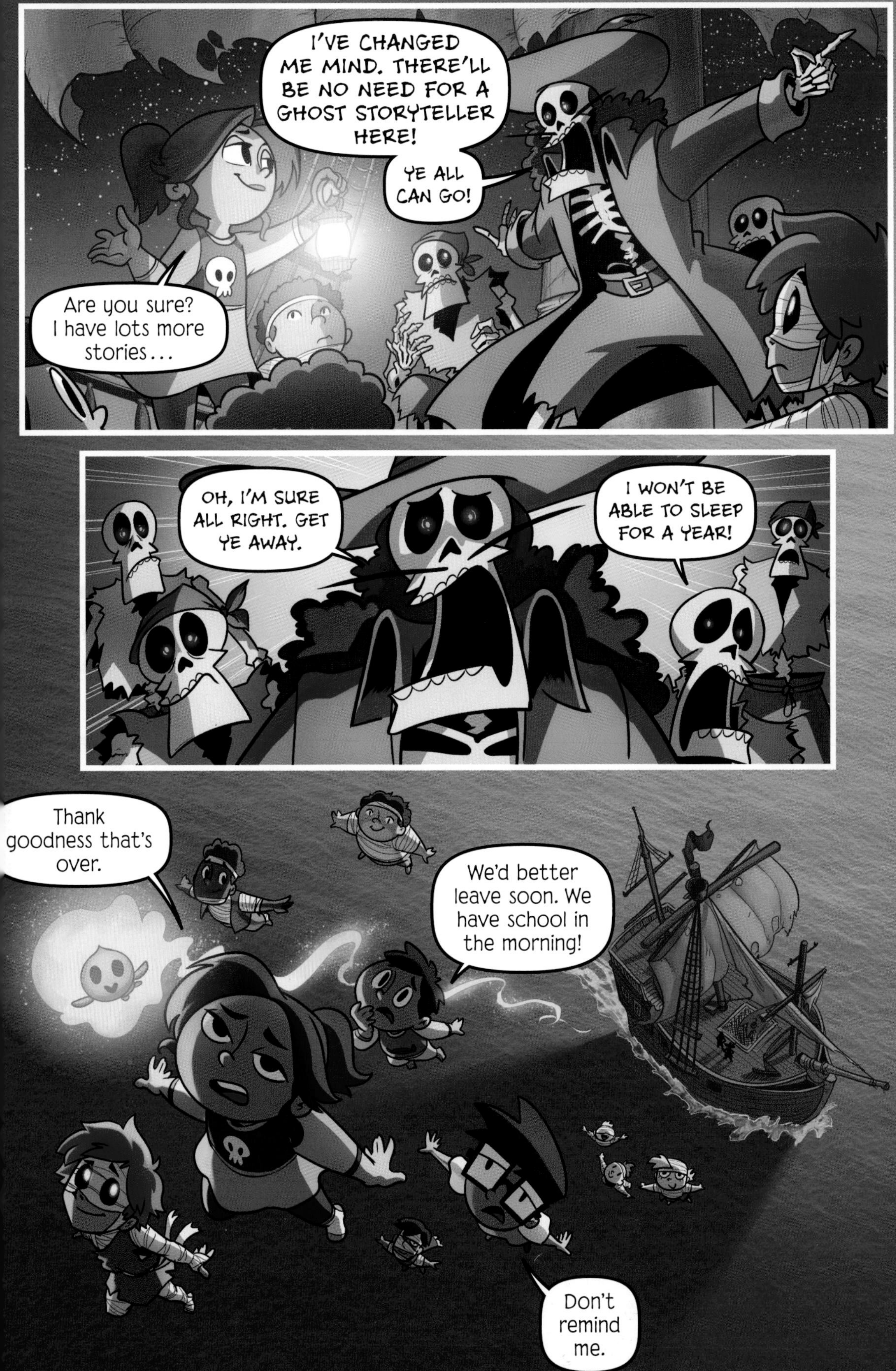
I'VE CHANGED ME MIND. THERE'LL BE NO NEED FOR A GHOST STORYTELLER HERE!
YE ALL CAN GO!
Are you sure? I have lots more stories...
OH, I'M SURE ALL RIGHT. GET YE AWAY.
I WON'T BE ABLE TO SLEEP FOR A YEAR!
Thank goodness that's over.
We'd better leave soon. We have school in the morning!
Don't remind me.

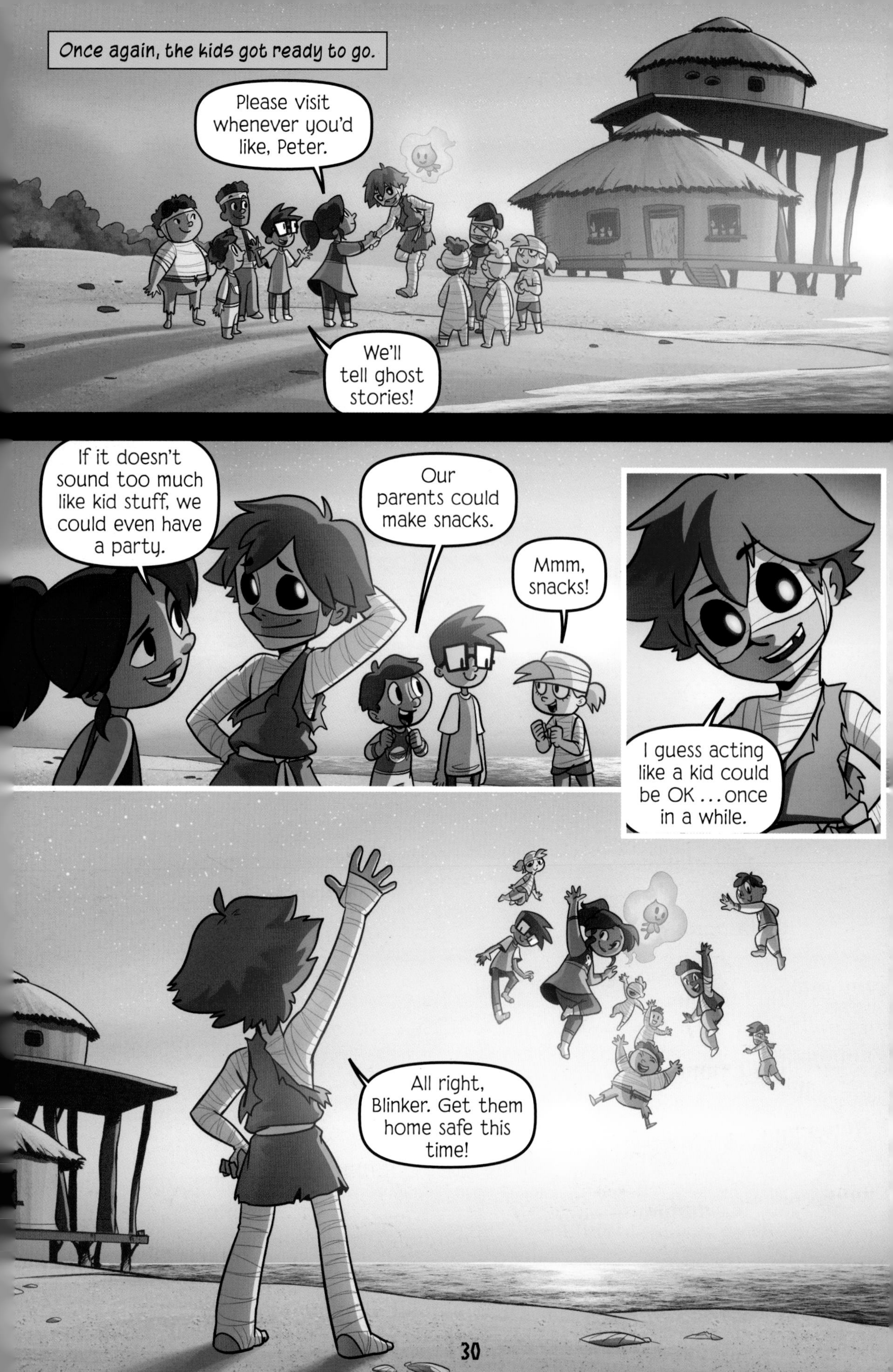

Once again, the kids got ready to go.
Please visit whenever you'd like, Peter.
We'll tell ghost stories!
If it doesn't sound too much like kid stuff, we could even have a party.
Our parents could make snacks.
Mmm, snacks!
I guess acting like a kid could be OK . . . once in a while.
All right, Blinker. Get them home safe this time!

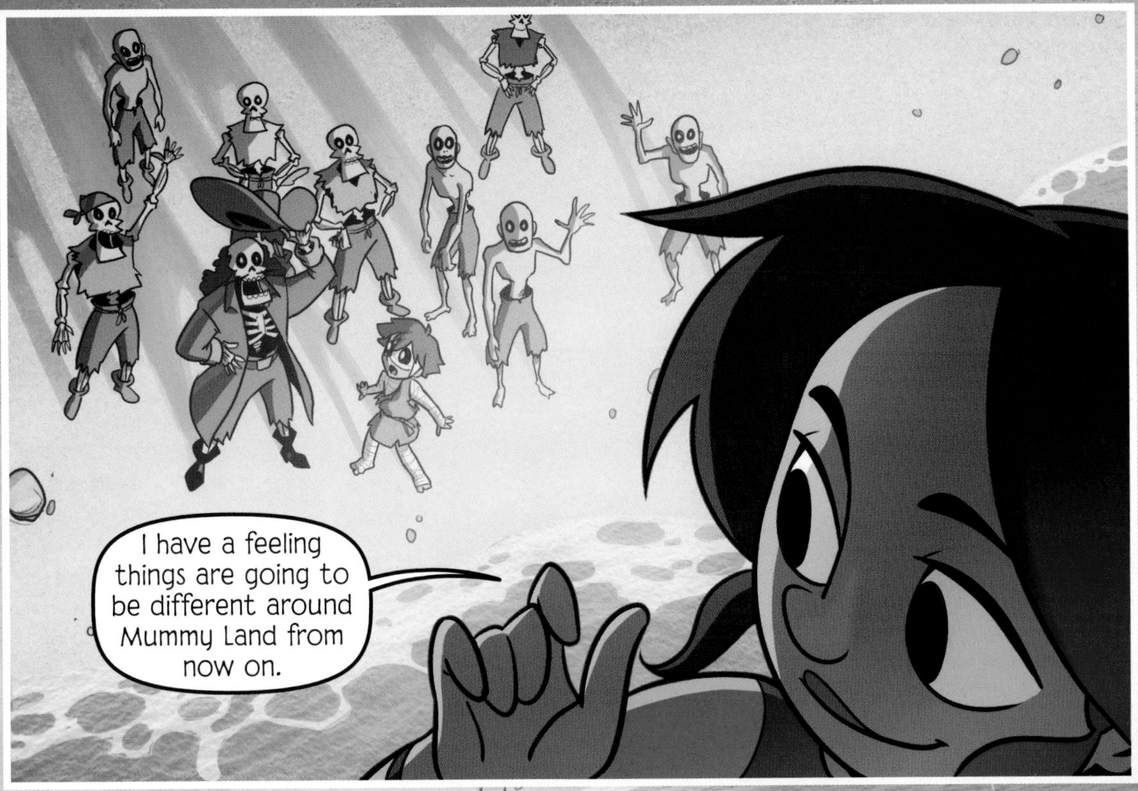
I have a feeling things are going to be different around Mummy Land from now on.

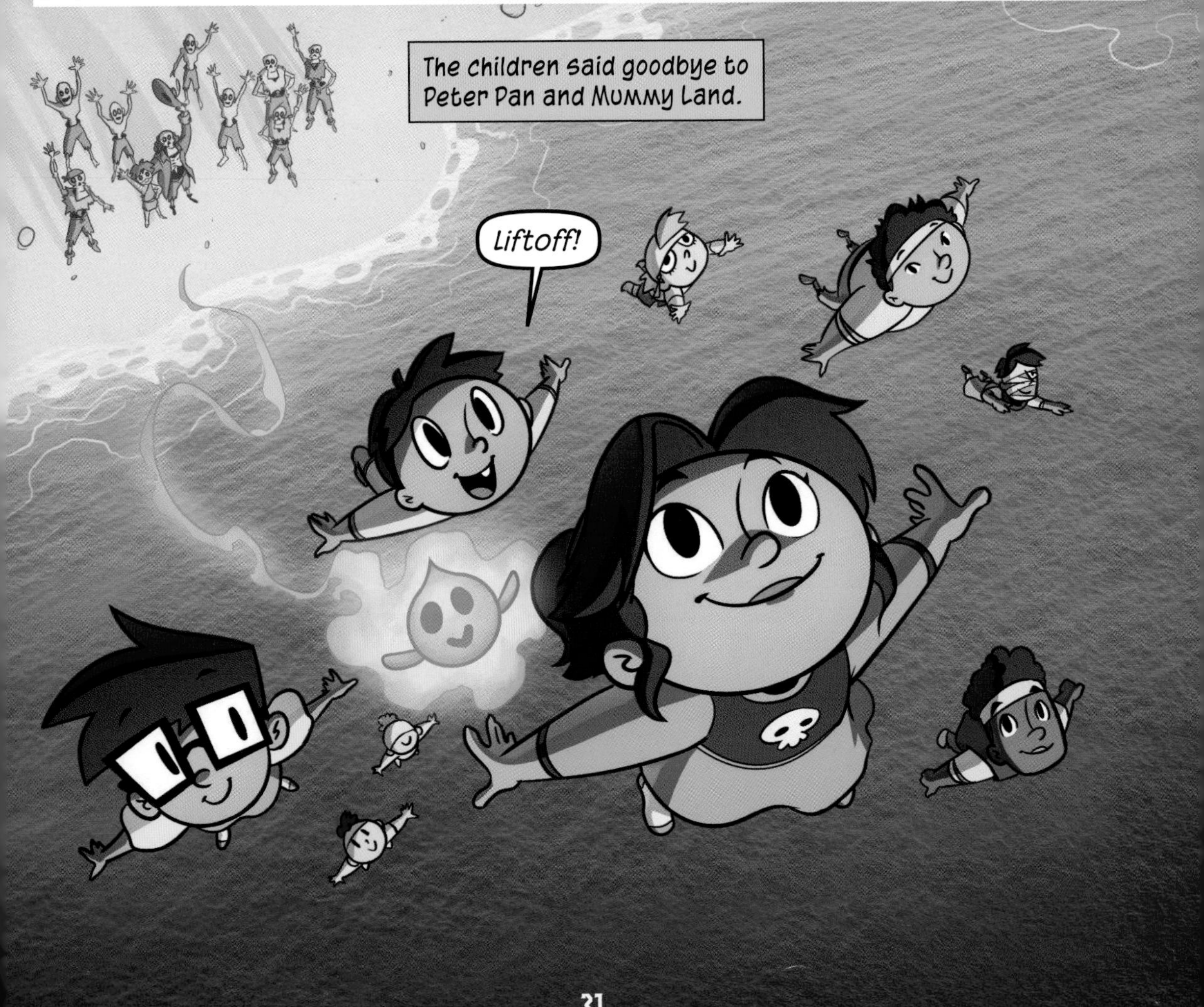
The children said goodbye to Peter Pan and Mummy Land.
Liftoff!

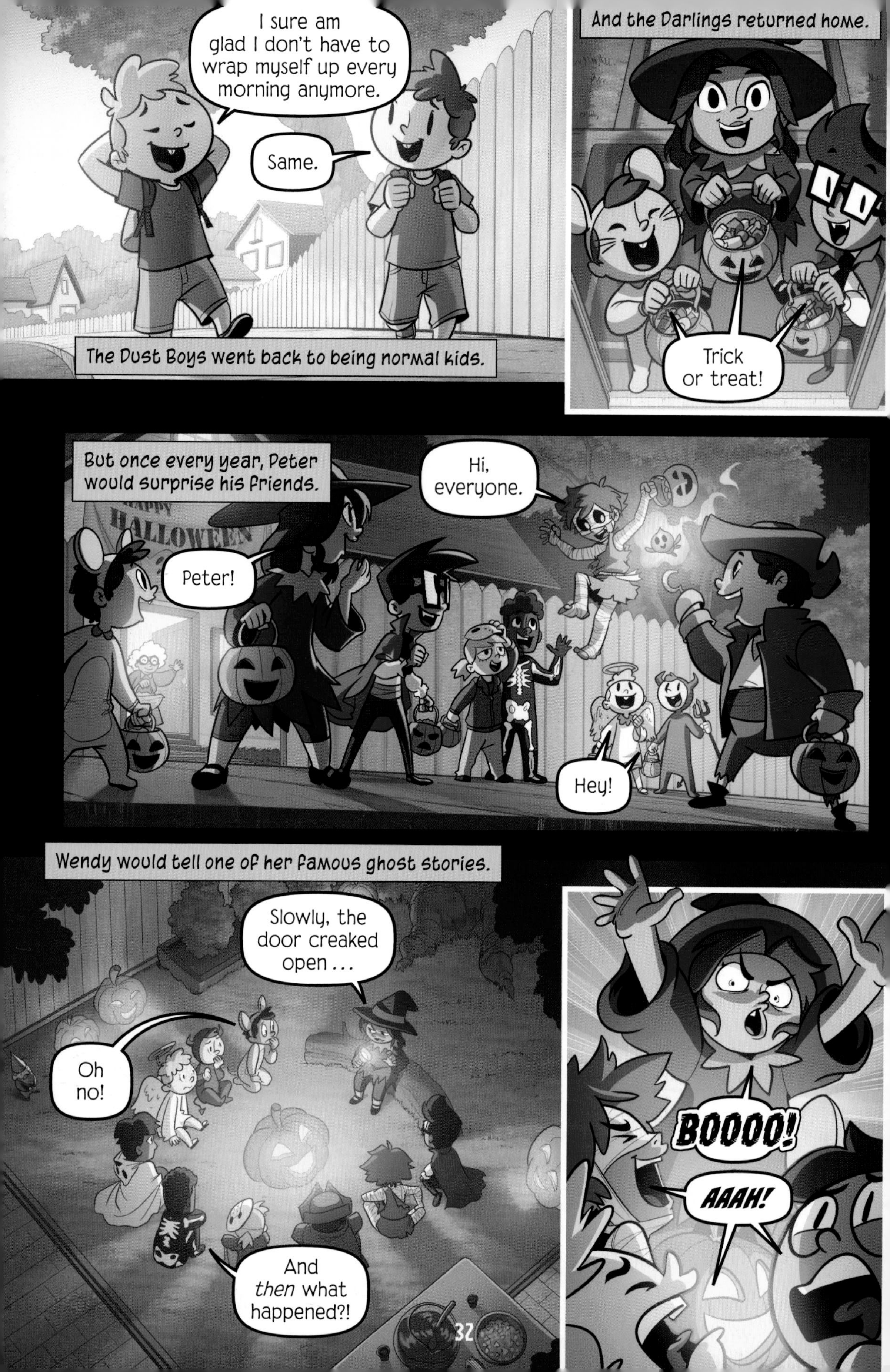

I sure am glad I don't have to wrap myself up every morning anymore.
Same.
The Dust Boys went back to being normal kids.
And the Darlings returned home.
Trick or treat!
But once every year, Peter would surprise his friends.
HAPPY HALLOWEEN
Hi, everyone.
Peter!
Hey!
Wendy would tell one of her famous ghost stories.
Slowly, the door creaked open . . .
Oh no!
And *then* what happened?!
BOOOO!
AAAH!

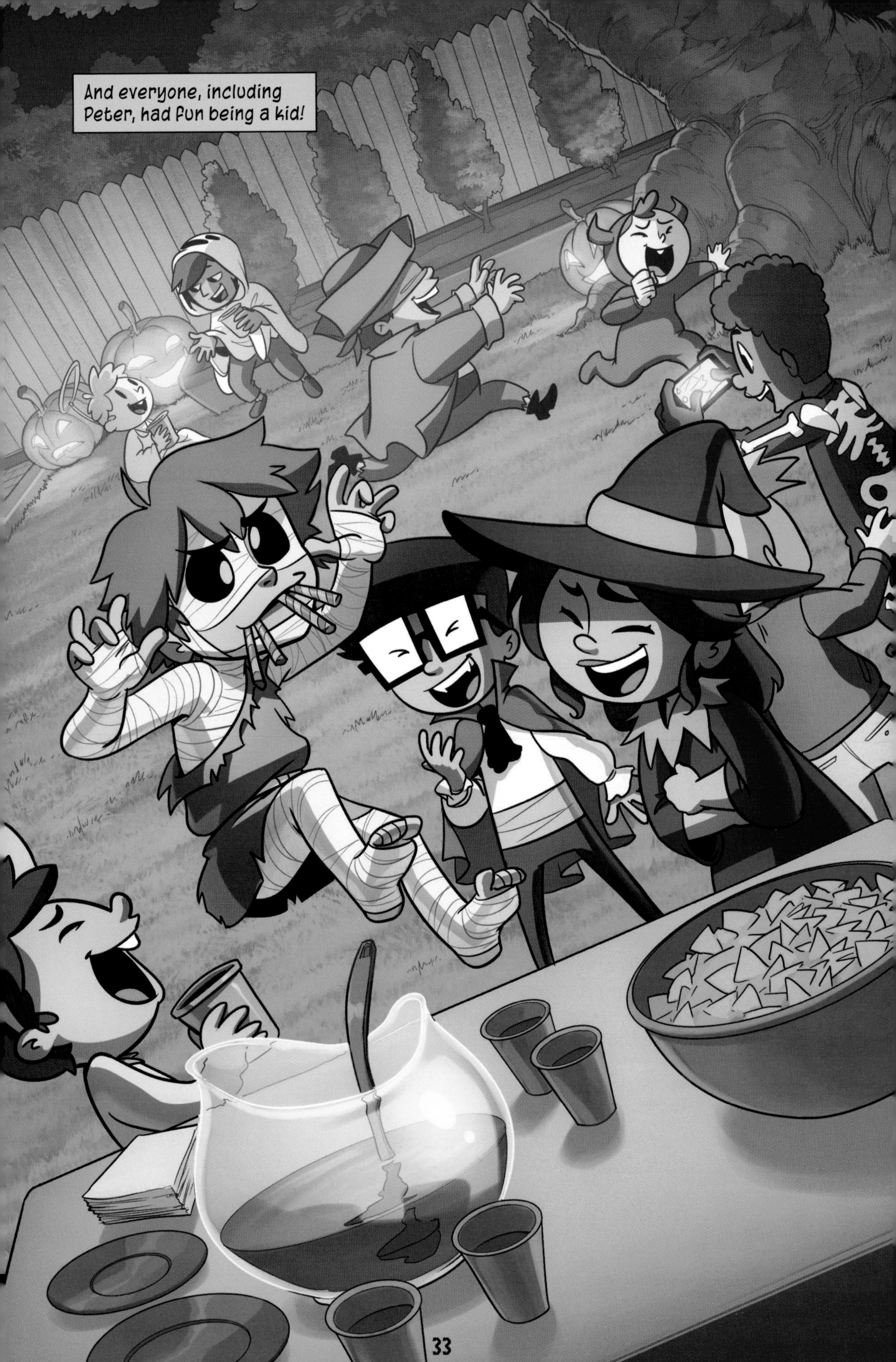
And everyone, including
Peter, had fun being a kid!

ALL ABOUT THE ORIGINAL STORY!

The character of
Peter Pan was created by
Scottish writer J.M. Barrie.
In 1904 Barrie published a play called
Peter Pan; or, The Boy Who Would Not Grow Up.
A few years later he wrote a novel called *Peter and Wendy.*

In the original, Peter Pan doesn't want to be old—instead he never wants to grow up! So he leaves home and goes to a magical place called Neverland where he will never age. There he lives with a fairy named Tinker Bell and the Lost Boys, kids who also ran away to keep from growing up.

Peter often visits the home of the Darlings. He loves to listen to the bedtime stories that Mrs. Darling tells to Wendy, John, and Michael. One night, Peter forgets his shadow at their house. When he comes back for it, Wendy spots Peter and helps him put the shadow back on. Peter is so impressed that he invites Wendy and her brothers to Neverland. He teaches them to fly and off they go.

The Darlings have many adventures on the island of Neverland with Peter, Tinker Bell, and the Lost Boys. But eventually they want to return home to their parents, and the Lost Boys decide to come with them. Peter, however, refuses to leave.

As the group heads out, a fierce pirate named Captain Hook captures them! He's called Hook because his hand was eaten by a crocodile, and he wears a hook in its place. He blames Peter for the injury and wants to hurt the boy back. Peter rushes to the pirate ship after learning about Hook's plans. Peter defeats his foe in a sword fight and rescues his friends. The Darlings and Lost Boys can now safely fly back home. Peter still stays behind, but he promises to visit them every spring.

A FAR OUT GUIDE TO
THE STORY'S MUMMIFIED TWISTS

In the original, Peter Pan is a boy who wants to be young forever. In this version, he's a mummy boy who wants to be old!

Peter's small flying friend is a fairy in the novel. Here she's a will-o'-the-wisp.

The original lagoon had mermaids swimming in its water. This one has plesiosaurs!

Instead of Wendy's mother telling bedtime stories, Wendy is telling ghost stories. And her terrifying tale saves the day!

VISUAL QUESTIONS

Wendy tells really scary stories. How does the art here help add to the spookiness?

1

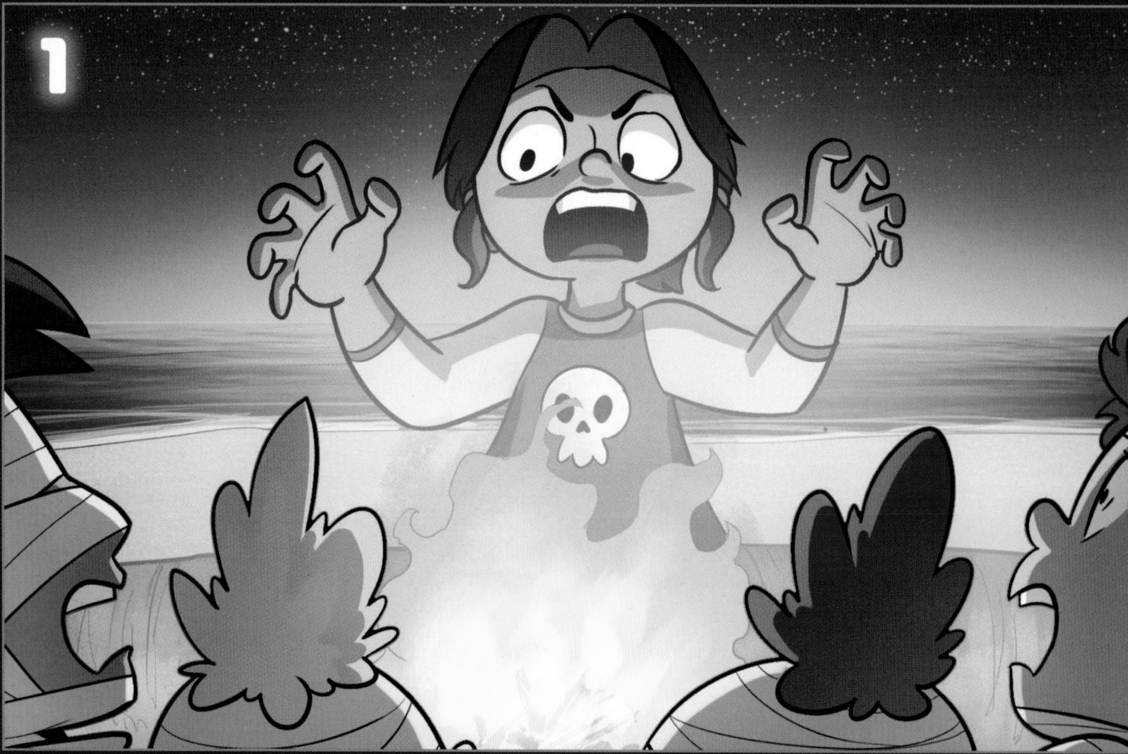

What's in these thought bubbles, and why are there red Xs through them? Describe how it connects with what Peter is saying.

2

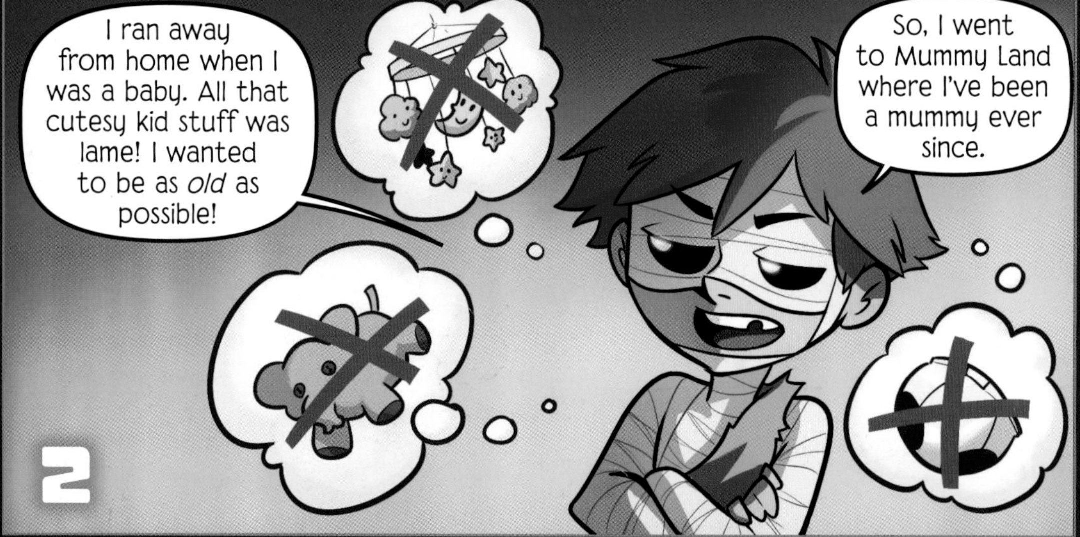

I ran away from home when I was a baby. All that cutesy kid stuff was lame! I wanted to be as *old* as possible!
So, I went to Mummy Land where I've been a mummy ever since.

Look at these panels from page 25. How do you think Peter feels about the Darlings and Dust Boys' decision to leave Mummy Land? What makes you think that?

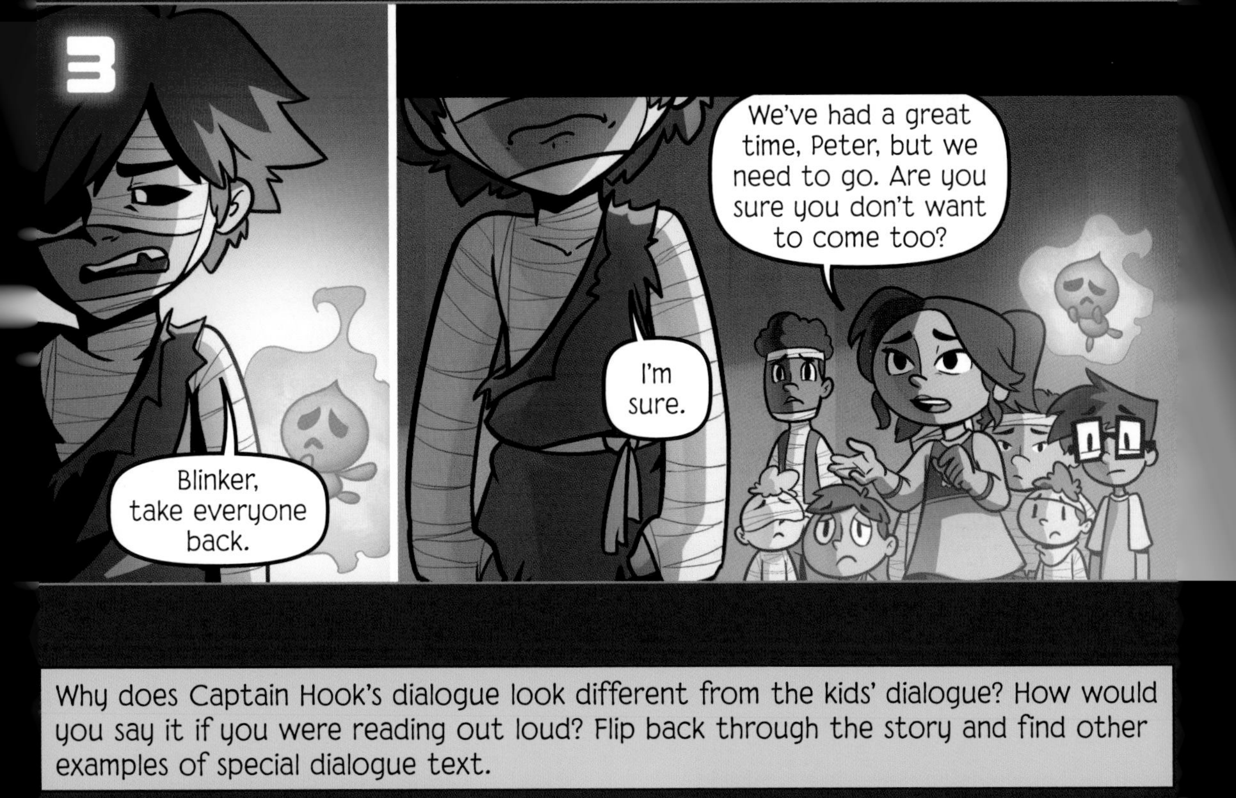
3
Blinker, take everyone back.
We've had a great time, Peter, but we need to go. Are you sure you don't want to come too?
I'm sure.

Why does Captain Hook's dialogue look different from the kids' dialogue? How would you say it if you were reading out loud? Flip back through the story and find other examples of special dialogue text.

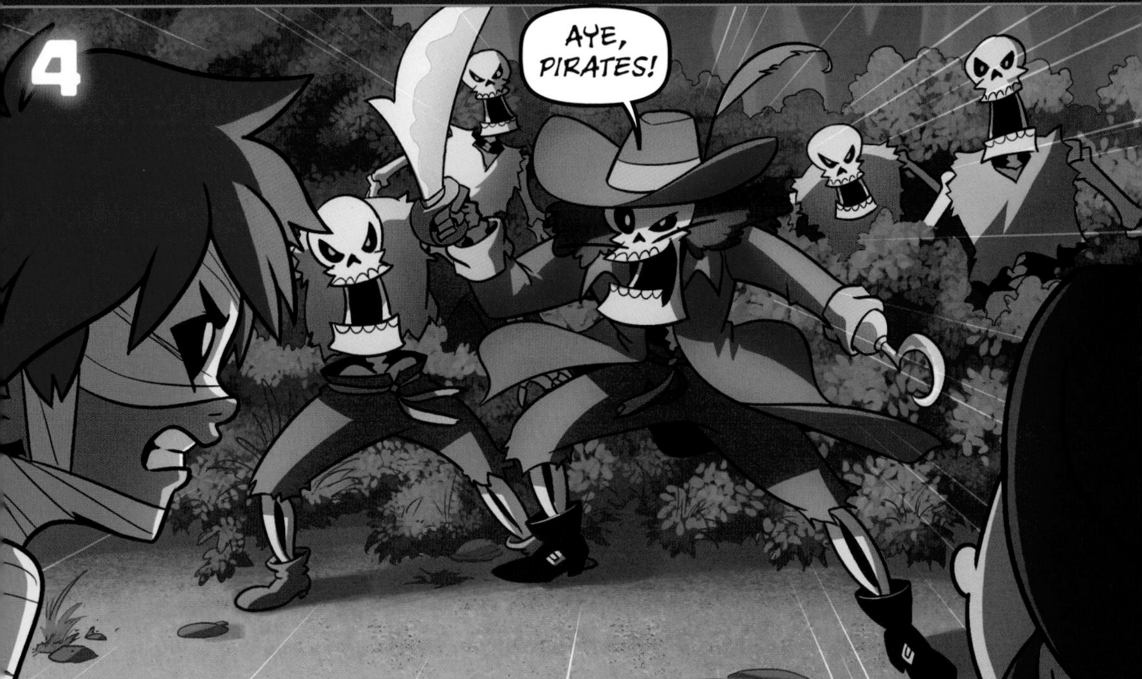
4
AYE, PIRATES!

AUTHOR

Benjamin Harper has worked as an editor at Lucasfilm LTD. and DC Comics. He currently lives in Los Angeles where he writes, watches monster movies, and hangs out with his cat, Edith Bouvier Beale, III. His other books include the Bug Girl series, *Obsessed with Star Wars*, *Rolling with BB-8*, and *Hansel & Gretel & Zombies*.

ILLUSTRATOR

Fern Cano is an illustrator born in Mexico City, Mexico. He currently resides in Monterrey, Mexico, where he makes a living as an illustrator and colorist. He has done work for Marvel, DC Comics, and role-playing games like Pathfinder from Paizo Publishing. In his spare time, he enjoys hanging out with friends, singing, rowing, and drawing!

GLOSSARY

bandage (BAN-dij)—a strip of cloth used to cover and protect parts of the body

double-crosser (DUH-buhl-KROS-uhr)—a person who cheats others by saying they will do one thing but then doing another

glide (GLAHYD)—to move in a smooth way

gloomy (GLOO-mee)—causing feelings of sadness

horde (HOHRD)—a large group of something (like zombies!)

lagoon (luh-GOON)—a small body of water between the shore and a coral reef

moan (MOHN)—to make a long, low sound, usually in pain or sadness

mummy (MUH-mee)—a dead body that has been kept from breaking down through the use of special salts and has been wrapped in bandages

terrifying (TER-uh-fahy-ing)—causing a great amount of fear

tomb (TOOM)—a room or building that holds dead bodies

unravel (uhn-RAV-uhl)—to come apart bit by bit

will-o'-the-wisp (wil-oh-thuh-WISP)—in folktales, a spirit that appears at night, often in wetlands, as a small light and tries to trick people into getting lost

OLD FAVORITES. NEW SPINS.

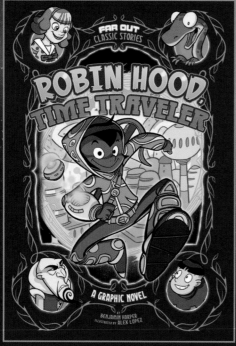

FAR OUT CLASSIC STORIES

ONLY FROM CAPSTONE!